Gabriel

Texts and Translations

The Text and Translations series was founded in 1991 to provide students and teachers with important texts not readily available or not available at an affordable price and in high-quality translations. The books in the series are intended for students in upper-level undergraduate and graduate courses in national literatures in languages other than English, comparative literature, ethnic studies, area studies, translation studies, women's studies, and gender studies. The Texts and Translations series is overseen by an editorial board composed of specialists in several national literatures and in translation studies.

For a complete listing of titles, see the last pages of this book.

GEORGE SAND

Gabriel
An English Translation

Translated by Kathleen Robin Hart and
Paul Fenouillet

Introduction by Kathleen Robin Hart

The Modern Language Association of America
New York   2010

MLA and the MODERN LANGUAGE ASSOCIATION are trademarks owned
by the Modern Language Association of America. For information about
obtaining permission to reprint material from MLA book publications, send
your request by mail (see address below), e-mail (permissions@mla.org), or
fax (646 458-0030).

Library of Congress Cataloging-in-Publication Data

Sand, George, 1804–1876.
[Gabriel. English]
Gabriel : an English translation / George Sand ; translated [from the
French] by Kathleen Hart and Paul Fenouillet ; introduction by
Kathleen Hart.
p. cm. — (Texts and translations. [Translations], ISSN 1079-2538 ; 28)
Includes bibliographical references and index.
ISBN 978-1-60329-078-4 (pbk. : alk. paper)
1. Sex role—Drama. I. Hart, Kathleen, 1960– II. Fenouillet, Paul, 1961–
III. Title.
PQ2396.G3713 2010
842'.7—dc22   2010024988

Texts and Translations 28
ISSN 1079-2538

Cover illustration: Photograph of Sarah Mesguich, by Bruno Dewaele,
from a production of *Gabriel* in Paris in 2002

Printed on recycled paper

Published by The Modern Language Association of America
26 Broadway, New York, New York 10004-1789
www.mla.org

CONTENTS

Acknowledgments

"Never work completely alone" is a cardinal rule of translation. We sought the assistance and advice of many people, who deserve our special thanks. For their editorial assistance, we thank Margit Longbrake, Michael Kandel, David Nicholls, and also Cynthia Kerr, a friend and colleague. We thank the librarians of Vassar College for locating so many of the works Kathleen Robin Hart consulted and for patiently indulging her frequent requests to renew items already overdue. John Ahern provided helpful information on the Italian language, while Rachel Kitzinger generously shared her knowledge of classical Roman myth and legend. Donald Foster and Zoltan Markus gave us their expert advice on seventeenth-century English language and theater. David Powell, Karen Offen, Lucienne Frappier-Mazur, and Françoise Genevray contributed to the critical bibliography. For their insightful comments on various parts of the manuscript, we thank Gabrielle Cody, William

J. Harrington, John Huttlin, Karen Offen, David Powell, Christine Reno, and the anonymous reviewers for the Modern Language Association. The late Frank Paul Bowman also commented on the manuscript in its early stages. We dedicate this project to his memory.

INTRODUCTION

"Strange that the most virile talent of our time should be a woman's!" (H. L. 1).[1] Such critical assertions of the greatness of George Sand were common in the 1830s, notwithstanding frequent caricatures of her in the popular press as a promiscuous, cigar-smoking woman in trousers. No other woman of the period was represented more often in paintings and lithographs, or so reviled and celebrated, alternately, as much for how she lived as for what she wrote.[2] Sand knowingly cultivated a unique public persona that distinguished her from both male and female writers; yet her unconventional appearance and conduct were no mere props to her fame. Like the name George that she used in her private life, they were expressions of a deeply ingrained alternative gender identity, which writing allowed her to assert more freely.

Born Amandine Aurore Lucile Dupin in 1804, George Sand was the daughter of an aristocratic father, Maurice Dupin, and a commoner, Sophie Delaborde.[3] When Maurice died suddenly in 1808, Sophie resumed work as a dressmaker in Paris, leaving her daughter in the custody of Maurice's mother at the château of Nohant in Berry. There the young Aurore was trained by her grandmother to adopt "all sorts of seemingly ridiculous manners" required of a "lady" (Sand, *Story* 490). Yet she was also instructed in a variety of subjects by her father's tutor, at a time when most girls received little or no real schooling.[4] On returning to Berry from a convent in her teen years, she devoted herself to serious reading and learned to straddle a horse. Encouraged by the eccentric tutor, named Deschartres, she rode the estate horses daily through the countryside, dressed in a man's frock coat. Thus she enjoyed unusual independence as a girl, but her options as an adult were more limited. Considered overemotional, intellectually inferior, and even somewhat infirm, women were barred from most professions or participation in civic life.[5] In 1822, at the age of nineteen, Aurore married Baron François Casimir Dudevant, with whom she had a son, Maurice, and a daughter, Solange.

As her relationship with Casimir deteriorated, Sand began to contemplate writing as a vocation. Few married women of her day could have pursued that goal. The Napoleonic Civil Code, drawn up between 1800 and 1804, had codified the subordination of women to men in a uniform body of laws, and in 1816 it prohibited divorce.[6] But Casimir reluctantly agreed to a legal separation, and in 1831 Sand moved to Paris, eventually bringing the children with her. Her first publications were articles, short stories, and two novels written in collaboration with the writer Jules Sandeau. It was during this time that Sand began dressing as a man on a regular basis. She reveled in the pleasure of mobility so drastically inhibited by the voluminous skirts, corsets, and flimsy shoes of women's styles; in sturdy boots, she "flew from one end of Paris to the other" (*Story* 893). Masculine attire suited her temperament, which eschewed the self-conscious gestures and poses associated with the prevailing norms of femininity. Though technically in violation of a police regulation that prohibited cross-dressing, Sand could pass for a man and go places off-limits to women, such as the theater pit.[7]

Sand's male disguise extended to her adoption of a masculine authorial voice for her first independently written novel, *Indiana*, which appeared in 1832 under the name "G. Sand." Many women authors resorted to a male pseudonym to gain access to a literary market increasingly hostile to women. Sand deftly assumed the voice of a male narrator who at times disparages "the other sex" yet sympathizes with the eponymous heroine, who revolts against a tyrannical husband.[8] In this manner, Sand delivered a forceful critique of women's subjugation without appearing to speak as a woman. Critics praised "Monsieur Sand" with enthusiasm, and the novel went through three new editions in four months before most people had learned that its author was actually female. Having established herself as a major new literary talent, she settled on the first name George. As fascination with the author's double-gender identity grew, newspapers and periodicals took to featuring Sand in articles and illustrations, which in turn heightened public interest in her novels.

Public speculation about her love affairs did not always give Sand an advantage. The male-dominated press already treated women authors as suspect for straying into

the public sphere. Political conservatives found Sand's independent lifestyle especially offensive and attacked her
writings as shockingly critical of marriage and the Catholic Church. With the eruption of a wave of feminist pro-
test in the 1830s, stereotypes of the feminist had merged
with those of the woman writer: both types were portrayed in the masculine press as narcissistic, immoral, and
unoriginal. Hostile male critics, including rival novelists,
were inclined to denigrate Sand's character and talent in
the same breath and to insinuate that her novels were
thinly veiled accounts of her own depraved amorous ad-
ventures. These factors may explain why Sand distanced
herself from feminist groups and frequently downplayed
the relation between her works and her personal life.[9] At
stake was her reputation as a serious artist.

"Rarely does the fantasy of artists correspond directly
to their actual situation," she states in the preface to a
new 1854 edition of *Gabriel*.[10] But if such a link is not direct, it remains indirect. Affirming the artist's need to
escape the oppressive real world, the preface calls attention to what it seems to belie: art gives Sand the freedom
to exalt a transgressive gender identity.[11] Through her
creation of the heroically virtuous Gabriel, the artist can
aestheticize the tragically real consequences of masculine
domination.

The drama unfolds in seventeenth-century Italy, when
Gabriel is seventeen. The reader learns that Gabriel's
grandfather, Jules, the prince of Bramante, quarreled
long ago with his younger son, Octave, and determined
that his elder son, Julien, should inherit his wealth and

title of prince.[12] At the time, property and wealth could go only to male offspring, and the rule of agnatic succession excluded females from inheriting a throne.[13] Thus, when both Julien and his wife unexpectedly died, leaving behind no male heir but only a baby girl, Jules instructed the nanny and the tutor to raise the girl, named Gabriel, as a boy. We learn in the prologue that the upbringing has apparently succeeded. By age seventeen, Gabriel excels at Latin and Greek, fences brilliantly, and enjoys riding and hunting. Jules, to consolidate his "grandson's" masculine identity, has also ordered the tutor to instill in Gabriel the belief that women are weak, abject creatures. After Jules tells Gabriel the truth, which Gabriel has already suspected, Gabriel cries, "An admirable ruse, indeed! To inspire in me the horror of women, only to throw it in my face and say, But this is what you are." Though Gabriel is speaking of his own peculiar position, his words poignantly describe the experience of all women who have been socialized to devalue themselves.[14]

Gabriel's response to his predicament is that of a paradigmatic Romantic hero. Repulsed by the corrupt Jules, Gabriel nobly seeks out and befriends his cousin Astolphe, the son of Octave and rightful heir. This development allows Sand to develop a multifaceted critique of women's lack of freedom. Significantly, one of Gabriel's first traumas after learning his true sex occurs when, accompanied by Astolphe, he attends a carnival celebration disguised as a woman. Alone in his room wearing feminine garb for the first time, Gabriel laments his loss of physical freedom: "Everything binds and stifles me. This corset is torture, and I feel so awkward!" His discomfort contrasts with Astolphe's thrilled reaction to his appearance: "[W]hen you are in that costume, I feel a passion for you that is jealous, ardent, fearful, and chaste. Surely I shall never feel this way again." Homoerotic or not,[15] Astolphe's love for Gabriel is extraordinary, because Astolphe is attracted to the man in her as well as the woman. Before learning her secret, he muses, "I would like to have a mistress who looks like him. But a woman can never have that kind of beauty, that mix of candor and strength. . . ." On learning that Gabriel is in fact female, Astolphe is overjoyed.

Sand's play invites us to wonder whether patriarchal culture, which opposes masculine to feminine comportment, deprives us of the kind of intimate partner we may yearn for most. Unaccustomed to treating women as equals, Astolphe eventually can no longer tolerate his cousin's autonomy and intellectual prowess. "Could you not be a woman?" he entreats her. The implication of such episodes is that gender is socially constructed rather than determined by nature.[16] Yet Gabriel(le) is not simply a courageous and intelligent masculine hero who happens to be anatomically female. Rather, s/he is androgynous. "I do not feel that my soul has a sex," s/he declares.[17] Gabriel(le) possesses many traits or talents aligned with femininity: tenderness of heart, a horror of blood, and an artistic sense, as evidenced by his/her poetic talent for dressing and embroidery. Gabriel(le) displays the best qualities traditionally associated with each sex.[18]

Literary representations of androgyny had been in vogue during the 1830s, which saw the publication of Henri de Latouche's *Fragoletta* (1829), Honoré de Balzac's

Séraphita (1835), and Théophile Gautier's *Mademoiselle de Maupin* (1835). These examples may have inspired Sand to link androgyny with transvestism, itself a popular theme of theater and literature. But Pierre Leroux's Romantic socialism, which Sand both embraced and helped articulate, may also have inspired *Gabriel*. Leroux held that all human beings possessed the three faculties of sensation, sentiment, and knowledge; only when all men and women actuated those faculties in themselves would a truly egalitarian society emerge.[19] From this perspective, Gabriel(le) is the ideal human being, for s/he is at once compassionate, highly educated, and athletic. Inevitably, s/he is a tragic hero(ine), because a rigidly hierarchical society cannot accommodate such an individual.[20] Astolphe remarks, "You were born endowed with all faculties, all virtues, all graces, and you are misunderstood!" Sand takes up the Romantic theme of the sensitive, misunderstood individual to glorify an androgynous character's struggle against the rigid enforcement of gender roles.

The literary depiction of an exceptional female character's struggle with women's legal and social subjection was not new; one finds it in other novels by Romantic women writers, including earlier works by Sand.[21] What particularly distinguishes *Gabriel* is the correlation between its subject matter—the travails of a character neither altogether male nor female—and its hybrid generic status as neither altogether play nor novel. Its unwieldy prose and overall length detract from its dramatic force; yet the onstage sword fights, local color, multiple settings, and slang combine to ally *Gabriel* strongly with the aims of Romantic theater, which sought to bring a new vitality to the stage.[22] Though she dubbed it a "novel in dialogue," Sand wished fervently to have *Gabriel* performed. She nourished a lifelong passion for theater: not only did she write, produce, and direct plays; she also designed costumes and published essays on acting and theater practice. In addition to writing twenty-five plays that premiered in Parisian professional theaters, she wrote and staged plays at her private theater at Nohant (with music occasionally provided by her lover, the composer and pianist Frédéric Chopin). Alfred de Musset's play *Lorenzaccio* (1834) was based on the initial sketch of a play that Sand wrote entitled *A Conspiracy in 1537 (Une conspiration en 1537)*. She published her second play, *Aldo the Rhymer (Aldo le rimeur)*, in 1833 and her third play, *The Seven Strings of the Lyre (Les sept cordes de la lyre)*, in 1838.

Gabriel belongs to the first, Romantic phase of Sandian drama.[23] We might call these works closet dramas, provided we keep in mind that a closet drama was not necessarily intended only for readers. Romantic playwrights had already won their battle against the procedural codes of classical tragedy, but the large middle-class audience of the July Monarchy was not interested in what it perceived as antisocial, antibourgeois themes, especially feminist ones (Daniels 17). Closet dramas, including Musset's collection "Armchair Theater" (*Un spectacle dans un fauteuil*), enabled Romantic playwrights to experiment with new dramatic ideas and make them immediately available to the reading public. In some cases, the publication of closet dramas made audiences more receptive to their staging later on.

The generic instability of *Gabriel* is symptomatic of Sand's reaching beyond the theatrical conventions and social realities of her time, but in a way that specifically relates to the theme of gender instability. Though written in dramatic form, *Gabriel* has generic properties of the sentimental social novel, of which Sand was a major practitioner. The subgenre can be traced to an eighteenth-century feminine tradition of sentimental novel writing that depicted the protracted inner struggle of a character torn between individual freedom and collective welfare. In a typical scenario, the female protagonist is tragically unable to resolve the ethical dilemma that pits honest expression of her true feelings against familial duties. In the 1830s, however, considerable tensions surrounded the question of how to define the collective welfare. Sentimental novels depicted the prevailing social order and its institutions as corrupt and harmful, especially to the poor and the powerless, including women. Politically engaged writers wrote fiction suggesting that an ethical choice might be to reject the existing order. To readers who shared these writers' moral standards, a culturally rebellious character could be seen as virtuous.[24]

Gabriel depicts the tragic conflict a woman experiences between her desire to engage in gender-inappropriate behaviors and her need to meet familial obligations. Though family is traditionally associated with collective welfare, in *Gabriel* the characters representing familial duties are flawed or corrupt. The stone-hearted Prince Jules, the lewd Brother Como, the spiteful Settimia, and the despotic Astolphe all selfishly attempt to suppress in Gabriel(le) the behaviors they consider inappropriate for the gender role they wish him/her to play, thereby compromising his/her integrity. Gabriel, by contrast, is motivated by ethical considerations at every turn; even Gabriel's quest for freedom is tied to a concern for others and for the truth. The gravity of the play's rhetoric is meant to engage readers with Gabriel's eminently virtuous struggle against rigidly enforced gender roles. Tragically, no course of action can rescue Gabriel from the agony of dissimulation.

Sand could not expect her male readers to appreciate the significance of such a struggle. Nor could she count on readers to respond positively to an unmarried heroine who lives with her lover, travels in male circles, shoots a man with her pistol, and wields a sword. A just appreciation of Sand's ingenuity requires that we consider not only her era's aesthetic tastes, which ran to the hyperbolic, but also the critical expectation that works by women would evince feminine sentimentality. At the time Sand wrote *Gabriel*, a growing contingent of realist writers and critics were seeking to discredit the sentimental paradigm in favor of novels depicting protagonists who pursued self-gratification in an individualistic and competitive society. Yet male critics still expected women writers to extol the virtues of womanly self-sacrifice and to display a feminine literary style. Because realist codes were beginning to triumph over a sentimental poetics of inflated diction and moral absolutism, women writers were placed in "a compromised position" (M. Cohen 163–95). Increasingly compared unfavorably with realist authors, women writers were nonetheless constrained by publishers and critics to write as women.

Sand found a way around this double bind. Her unparalleled critical and commercial success as a woman author owes much to her genius for a certain sleight of hand. Knowing she will be judged as a woman first and a writer second, she cunningly appropriates stock situations to serve radical ends. She bows to convention in some places while subverting it in others. While indulging in feminine mawkishness on many a page, she surreptitiously expresses sentiments of quite another order.

Gabriel remarkably illustrates this hit-and-run strategy. In act 3, scene 5, Settimia has just castigated Gabrielle in the name of self-sacrificing motherhood. Alone with Astolphe, Gabrielle resembles the quintessential self-sacrificing wife when, hoping to restore family harmony, she offers to give up horseback riding. Yet her feminine display of altruism is precisely what incites Astolphe to deplore the extreme sacrifices wives are expected to make:

> I would be a scoundrel if I forgot what you sacrificed for me by wearing the clothes of your sex and giving up the freedom, the active life, the noble occupations of the mind that you enjoyed and were used to. Give up your horse? Alas! It is the only exercise that has saved your health from the decline that was brought on by the change in your ways and that was beginning to worry me.

For all that it may strike modern ears as exaggerated and formulaic, Astolphe's speech gives a new and explosive interpretation to the virtue of feminine sacrifice, suggesting it frequently serves ignoble purposes. His own emphatic words pave the way for Gabriel to appear virtuous when she later escapes from him, as he indeed becomes a scoundrel bent on destroying her freedom.

Gabriel's inordinate length and prosy speeches testify to the great challenge Sand faced to make her main character sympathetic to a preeminently antifeminist audience. Like many Romantic authors, she did not see the need for economy in dramatic action and dialogue. In 1840, her first staged play, *Cosima*, which also probes the

cultural devaluation of women, was a colossal failure
that left her emotionally devastated. Inexperience alone,
however, cannot explain the gap between intention and
result, if we consider that the closet drama was often a
means by which Romantic playwrights reached for a theater of the future.[25] *Gabriel*'s elaborate speeches take on a
tragic dimension in counterpoint to features of the play
that maximize the resources of the stage. Sand's theme
that gender is a matter of performance and costume is reinforced by her chosen genre: theater. That Gabriel must
learn first the male and then the female role suggests
that playacting, the practice of dressing and behaving as
a man or woman, is not limited to the stage.[26] While this
notion certainly resides in other plays that feature cross-
dressing,[27] it usually serves as the basis for comedy or
as a pretext for lewdness. *Gabriel* alone renders the phe-
nomenon tragic, while delivering a sustained critique of
socially constructed gender roles that engages every as-
pect of theater, from plot and dialogue to costume and
characterization.[28]

It is for this reason, more than for its explicitly feminist themes, that *Gabriel* seems uncannily modern. The
period costumes do not merely create a reality effect or
entertain the senses; they effectively convey the arbitrari-
ness of gender codes.[29] The male costumes announce that
ornament and color were not always coded female in an
era preceding what J. C. Flügel called "the Great Masculine Renunciation," which took place after the French
Revolution, when male attire became dark and austere.[30]
Costume also raises questions about the virtue of con-
forming to gender codes, when Gabriel exclaims over

the indecency of her first dress, which bares her wrists and neckline. The looser-fitting doublet allows her modestly to conceal her body's shape.[31] When Antonio wants Gabriel to remove the doublet, Gabriel proves her/his manhood by dint of how well s/he uses a sword. Sand uses both costume and stage action to create a double-gendered individual who simultaneously upholds female honor, defined as bodily privacy, and masculine honor, defined as heroic courage. Defending one's honor is loosened from its gender-specific meanings and redefined as the fundamentally human quest for dignity and self-determination.[32]

The theme of carnival also underscores Sand's radical conceptualization of gender as masquerade and make-believe. Carnival celebrations took place during the ten days before Lent, the period before Easter when Catholics refrain from eating meat (the word *carnival* probably comes from the Latin *carnelevarium*, meaning "to remove meat"). Derived from ancient pagan rites (and Bacchic revelries), the carnival tradition of donning masks and celebrating wildly became extremely popular in Europe during the fifteenth and sixteenth centuries, particularly in Italy. The most common carnival costume, worn by Astolphe, Faustina, and Gabriel in act 5, scenes 3 and 4, was the domino, a garment also worn to the masked balls at the Opéra, which were a major form of Parisian entertainment in Sand's era. Hinting of adventure and intrigue, the typical domino consisted of a sweeping dark cloak accompanied by an elaborate mask.

The carnival costumes become visual tropes of the mystery surrounding Gabriel's ambiguous sexual identity that keeps the spectators in suspense. At the same time, the carnival theme participates in the subversion of traditional masquerade through what Pratima Prasad calls "a series of reversals" (341). Whereas *masquerade* usually connotes a false exterior that contrasts with the true identity concealed beneath it, Gabriel disguises himself as a woman in act 1 when in fact his body is female. Hence, "exterior costume, whether masculine or feminine, is always already a travesty." Anticipating the contemporary gender theories of Judith Butler and Marjorie Garber, the play demonstrates that all men and women play roles for which they must dress the part: "Transvestism does not transgress or cross, but enacts gender" (Prasad 342).

Was the play's challenge to prevailing ideologies of gender too disturbing for its own time and subsequent eras?[33] Though she considered *Gabriel* one of her finest works, Sand never lived to see it staged.[34] Between 1851 and 1855, she reduced the play's length and tried repeatedly to have it performed by various theater groups. Anticipating a negative reaction to the play's unusual premise, she prepared a version entitled *Julia*, which she "worked and reworked" in an effort to make it more palatable to the public (*Correspondance* 10: 425). Directors nonetheless objected to the play's length and the number of different sets it required, while actors were reluctant to play the unflattering role of Astolphe. But the play may in any event have been too unusual. We know from Sand's correspondence that at least one director refused to stage it for fear that the public would not understand it (10: 717). Or perhaps he feared that the public would understand it only too well.

We can rejoice that *Julia* did not replace what is presumably the bolder, more provocative version. Thanks to a more receptive sociopolitical climate, *Gabriel* has begun to receive the admiration and scholarly critical attention it deserves. Modern readers and spectators appreciate its critique of gender stereotypes, its ingenious plot twists, and scenes that are at once emotionally and visually engaging. Its power as theater has been confirmed by performances in the late twentieth and early twenty-first centuries (a briefer, modified version by Gilles Gleizes, entitled *Gabriel[le]*, was performed in Paris in the spring of 2002).[35] The time has come for the original, unadulterated version of *Gabriel* to take its rightful place alongside other, better-known works in the annals of great world literature.

Notes

[1] Unless otherwise indicated, all translations are mine.

[2] On nineteenth-century portraits and caricatures of Sand, see Bergman-Carton, esp. 19–64; Garval. Sand's continued status as a cultural icon is confirmed by numerous feature films about her, including James Papine's *Impromptu* (1990) and Diane Kury's *Children of the Century* (1999). On Sand's contemporary iconic status, see Massardier-Kenney 1–2.

[3] Harlan, a biographer, raises the possibility that Sand's biological father was a humble government employee and not Sophie Dupin's aristocratic husband (96–98).

[4] Women of Sand's privileged background did benefit from some private tutoring or from lessons at a convent, but schooling for girls emphasized "accomplishments" rather than academics (Moses 32–34; Rogers). Sand learned to paint, draw, and play the piano but also studied "boy's" subjects, including math, Latin, and natural history.

[5] The category of woman was naturalized in the works of eighteenth-century medical men and male philosophers (Steinbrügge; Laqueur).

However, the conceptualization of woman as a being sharply distinct from man did not emerge for the first time in the eighteenth century. Physician-philosophers' attempts to establish women's nature constituted the secularization of religious injunctions that previously had been used to justify keeping women in their place. These physician-philosophers' arguments were in actuality antifeminist responses to claims being made by women at the time that women's inferior education and legal subjection in marriage were the real cause of their ostensible inferiority (Offen, "Gender"; Park and Nye; and Stolberg). On women and the nineteenth-century medical establishment, see Burton; Kniebiehler.

[6]The civil code particularly restricted married women, who required their husbands' permission to dispose of property or exercise a profession. The husbands alone had legal authority over the offspring (see Moses 18–19; Burton). Sand's marriage took place during the politically repressive Restoration (the period from 1814 to 1830). She moved to Paris during the less reactionary July Monarchy (1830–48), which ushered in greater freedom of the press.

[7]Sand describes the details of her transition to wearing men's clothing in *Story of My Life* 892–93. Prohibitions against cross-dressing were not consistently enforced. In 1793, a group of revolutionary women complained to the National Convention that other female militants were trying to force them to wear the red cap of liberty. In response, Fabre d'Églantine gave a speech expressing fear that the red caps would be followed by women wearing pistol belts and "going for bread [as] men march to the trenches" (qtd. in Hunt 226). On 8 Brúmaire, year 2 (29 Oct. 1793), the National Convention ruled that "no person of either sex may constrain any citizen or citizeness to dress in a particular manner, each individual being free to wear whatever clothing or attire of his or her sex that pleases him, under pain of being suspect" (Duvergier 262). A ruling in 1800 (article 259) specifically required that women obtain legal permission if they planned to dress as men, and permission was given only for medical reasons. Just what constituted a legitimate medical reason was not specified, but according to Bard, women were allowed to cross-dress for reasons other than medical. Though archival evidence is scant, records show that some women obtained permission to cross-dress in order to exercise professions usually reserved for men; others obtained permission because they had masculine features, such as facial hair, that made them objects of curiosity if they wore female attire (3). The tension between expanding the right to dress freely on the one hand and curtailing the right to express one's gender identity

on the other hand continued until an 1853 French law explicity prohibited cross-dressing (Bard; Freadman; Nesci 245–60).

[8] For more on Sand's adoption of a male authorial voice, see Ezdinli; Powell.

[9] France was the birthplace of the first known autonomous women's movement in 1832 (Fraisse; Moses; and Riot-Sarcey). The words *feminist* and *feminism* "did not really enter public discourse until the end of the nineteenth century" (Offen, "On the French Origin" 47), but I use *feminist* to designate women's rights advocates. The most famous caricatures of feminists and bluestockings were published by the French artist and printmaker Honoré Daumier (1808–79) in the journals *La caricature* and *Le charivari* (Bergman-Carton; Walton). Sand was the target of especially harsh, scathing attacks after publishing her 1833 novel *Lélia* (Ezdinli 156–59). Many scholars have represented Sand as having negative or ambivalent attitudes toward feminism (Schor 68–81). But while keeping her distance from politically active women's groups, Sand sought to pave the way for future legal reforms by challenging, in her novels, cultural prejudices against women. She believed that before society could accept women in politics, it would first have to overturn oppressive marriage laws and recognize women's right to an education (Hart 91–99). Harkness dissects the pitfalls of equating Sand's political views with antifeminist statements made by various Sandian characters (or narrators).

[10] *Gabriel* was reprinted several times following its initial publication in *La revue des deux mondes*: it appeared in 1840 (Félix Bonnaire); in 1842, as part of her complete works (Perrotin); in 1848, as part of a new collection of complete works (Garnier frères); in another collection of some of her illustrated works, in 1854 (Hetzel); in 1867, with *Jean Zyska* (Michel Lévy); and again in 1988, with a preface by Janis Glasgow (Des femmes). Because the 1854 Hetzel edition appears in the aftermath of the failed 1848 revolution and Napoleon III's 1851 coup d'état, Sand may have found it especially prudent to claim in its preface that her play was pure fantasy.

[11] The preface in the French Romantic period allowed authors to play down the socially contentious content of their novels. This strategy was not lost on critics; as one of them remarked in 1832, "As a general rule, one knows that the very thing one denies in the preface is precisely what will show up throughout the book" (qtd. in Rossum-Guyon 81–82; this remark comes from a piece, signed "C. R.," in *Journal des débats* 21 July 1832). Glasgow observes that Sand's language does not truly dismiss the link between art and lived experience, though Glasgow does so to suggest Alfred de Musset as a model for Astolphe.

For an intriguing analysis of the character Gabriel in relation to Sand's metaphoric configurations of Chopin as angelic, see Kallberg. Sand's preface echoes in some ways Théophile Gautier's 1835 preface to *Mademoiselle de Maupin*, in which he famously espouses the credo of art for art's sake. An important difference, however, is that Gautier's celebration of art's autonomy is absolute, to the point that Gautier mocks utopian socialism and (ironically) derides any suggestion that art should serve a social purpose. Sand's preface leaves open the possibility that *Gabriel* is a work of social criticism. The preface contains another nod to Gautier in that passages of *Mademoiselle de Maupin* describe the ideal play, exemplified by Shakespeare's *As You Like It*, which Gautier's narrator says "makes one feel transported to an unknown world" and whose characters "rise above vulgar reality" (275). *Gabriel*, like Gautier's novel *Mademoiselle de Maupin*, might be drawing on the life of Julie Maupin (1670–1707, née d'Aubigny), a seventeenth-century cross-dressing swordswoman and opera star. Gabriel's duel with Antonio is a clever inversion of an anecdote about the real-life Maupin. Antonio wants Gabriel to prove his sex by removing his doublet, but Gabriel refuses. Julie Maupin was said to have bared her breasts to hecklers when they claimed she was too skilled with the sword to be a real woman (R. Cohen 80).

[12] The name Bramante calls to mind Bradamante, the heroic female knight of Ludovico Ariosto's *Orlando Furioso* (1516) and a recurrent mythical figure in Sand's writings (see Vierne 56–57).

[13] This rule obtained in most land-based aristocracies throughout Europe, though notable exceptions were the Netherlands, Austria, and Spain.

[14] To emphasize Gabriel's gender as situational, I use here the masculine or feminine pronoun according to whether Gabriel wishes to be considered male or female in a particular scene.

[15] Interestingly, Astolphe was the first name of a well-known homosexual writer of the time, Astolphe de Custine (1790–1857), whose salon Sand was known to have frequented.

[16] Astolphe is suggesting what Simone de Beauvoir would later famously argue in *The Second Sex*: "One is not born, but rather becomes a woman" (267), so that men can feel powerful and superior. The idea is not new: as early as the sixteenth century, early modern French critics of women's subordination repeatedly made distinctions between "nature" and "culture" (Offen, "Gender"). Particularly during the Enlightenment, "[c]ritiques of women's status provoked an awareness that the relations between the sexes were

neither God-given nor determined exclusively by Nature, but socially constructed; in other words, they understood the concept that we today call 'gender'" (Offen, "Reclaiming" 85).

[17] Sand was certainly familiar with the assertion often attributed to the author Madame de Staël (1766–1817) that "[g]enius has no sex," which itself echoes Poullain de la Barre's 1673 axiom that "[r]eason has no sex" (qtd. in Steinbrügge 12; the work by Poullain de la Barre is *De l'education des dames pour la conduite pour l'esprit dans les sciences et dans les mœurs* ["On the Education of Ladies for the Application of Their Minds to Scholarship and Manners"]).

[18] Through Gabriel, Sand gives a positive connotation to both equality and female difference, as evidenced by Gabriel's qualities and aptitude for skills coded feminine as well as those coded masculine. Fraisse shows how rhetorical constraints arising from specific historical circumstances affected the degree to which various feminists throughout the nineteenth century would emphasize equality with men or celebrate female difference.

[19] Many French Romantics proposed new meanings for the Christian Trinity. Leroux's ideas are inspired by the Saint-Simonian socialists, who held that each individual possessed three faculties: the rational, the motor, and the emotive. For more on Sand and Romantic socialism, see Naginski 138–89; Andrews.

[20] The rigidly hierarchical society is that of post-Renaissance Italy. In nineteenth-century France, wealth determined social prestige far more than lineage did. In each society, however, gender roles were rigidly enforced.

[21] Whereas the heroes of male-authored novels are usually portrayed as superior beings who take a melancholy pleasure in their voluntary withdrawal from society, the female heroines invented by Romantic women writers often experience social or romantic rejection as a result of their gender-inappropriate aspirations (Bertrand-Jennings; M. Cohen; Rabine; and Waller).

[22] French Romantic playwrights rejected the neoclassical theory of art that forbade violent action on stage. They upheld the rule of the three unities: unity of time, action, and place (Daniels).

[23] "Sand worked in the vanguard of three major movements: romanticism, realism, and the experimental little theater movement" (Manifold xvi).

[24] See M. Cohen 141–42. Modern readers might not perceive Sand's characters as rebellious. Male Romantic heroes could be more openly or consistently rebellious.

[25] "The closet drama sought the theater of the future," wrote Jeffrey N. Cox (qtd. in Cox 12). With *Cosima*, Sand had deliberately tried to challenge Parisian spectators with an unconventional play; she was aware that the public was threatened by its feminist content and the demands that long speeches placed on their patience. See her preface to *Cosima* in *Théâtre complet* 11–13. Also noteworthy is her "Essay on Fantastic Drama" ("Essai sur le drame fantastique"), published, like *Gabriel*, in 1839. Here, she argues that drama is enhanced when representations of inner struggle are juxtaposed with those of real-world events that contribute to such struggle and that through introspection the Romantic protagonist discovers an unknown world that is the "soul of all reality" (6). Later in her career, Sand transformed some of her novels into dramatic works that were successfully staged in Parisian theaters (Masson 111–13). Commenting on a new edition of her early dramatic works, an 1876 critic observes that Sand's dramatic heroines who "expatiate incessantly" are incomprehensible to the public and not suited for the stage (Garaguel 2).

[26] See Prasad for an extended discussion of gender as performance in relation to *Gabriel* and the theories of Judith Butler.

[27] One thinks particularly of Shakespeare's *As You Like It* and *Twelfth Night*. In both plays, a female character in male disguise travels about alone, wields a sword, and is attractive to unsuspecting women. Sand wrote a version of *As You Like It*, which she adapted to the stage in 1856. For more on Shakespeare as the most important model for French Romantic theater, see Daniels 16. Balzac once wrote Sand, "I have just read *Gabriel* for the first time, and I am delighted. It is a play by Shakespeare, and I do not understand why you have not had it staged" (Sand, *Correspondance* 5: 731).

[28] Berlanstein demonstrates that while cross-dressing was a "commonplace" in French plays before and after the Revolution, it most often expressed "silliness" in light musicals (341). During the nineteenth century, "male impersonation made very little use of its potential to turn the world upside down in a symbolic sense" (351). Cross-dress performances by women reinforced more than they challenged gender hierarchy as in *Vert-Vert* (1832), in which the actress Virginie Déjazet played a male youth who proves his mother was wrong to raise him in a convent as a girl, to prevent him from becoming like his violent father. By the nineteenth century it was too threatening to the ideal of masculine virility for men to impersonate women, and women almost always impersonated soft-skinned adolescent males, who were thought to be devoid of sexuality.

[29]Through costume and action, Sand practices a more modern semiotics of theater, approximating Ubersfeld's notion of "concrete theatrical space" as a "poetic object" "constructed in order to be a sign" that is both signifier and referent (102). The wearing of period costumes was standard practice in French Romantic theater. That Sand's characters wear period costumes is evident from the way they describe their own and one another's attire.

[30]Qtd. in Harvey 23. Beginning with the nineteenth century, Harvey traces the adoption of dark, austere clothing by men. According to Berlanstein, cross-dress performances in nineteenth-century French theater "reinforced the new elite's insistence on its own masculinity as well as on the femininity of the class that it was replacing." Female actresses playing aristocratic male youths in lace and knee breeches could "give symbolic support to the new ruling class," which liked to portray the old regime male aristocrat as frivolous and lacking in virility (356).

[31]Between Roman times and approximately 1620, women did not bare their wrists or lower arms. Though close-fitting in 1600, doublets were padded on the belly; by 1630 they resembled a loose jacket. Throughout the nineteenth century, female actresses dressing as men often appeared in trousers more revealing than what feminine attire allowed, providing "a cover for erotic pleasures that would otherwise have been suspect" (Berlanstein 339). Though erotic in its own ways, *Gabriel* thus avoids both the lewdness and frivolity of other plays that involved cross-dressing.

[32]His/her wish to cover up stems not from a prudish rejection of sexual feeling but from the need to protect a personal secret and avoid bodily violation. As soon as she appears in a dress, she becomes the object of unwanted attention and physical contact from Antonio. Nor is Gabriel's dueling a traditional expression of male honor; Gabriel pretends to be defending his masculine pride and ego, but his real motivation for fighting is to protect his secret and leave Rome quickly. For more on the tradition of dueling in relation to male honor, see Nye.

[33]Frenchwomen did not win the right to vote until 1944. Until the 1960s, married women were required to obtain permission from their husbands to work.

[34]"Of all of my manuscripts that I have reread, *Villemort le diable* is one of the worst and *Gabriel* is one of the best in subject matter" (Sand, *Correspondance* 17: 661). Sand wrote this letter in 1863 to the novelist and playwright Paul Meurice (1818–1905), with whom she cowrote three plays. On the following day, she

wrote Meurice another letter promising to send him a revised and radically shortened version of *Gabriel*, called *Octave*, which she had staged at Nohant in 1859 with friends and family. She states that those who performed *Octave* at Nohant lengthened or shortened the dialogue as they saw fit, and they even chose to end the play as they pleased.

[35]Interestingly, the Gleizes adaptation features the character of George Sand herself, who appears between certain scenes in order to narrate the details of what was cut from the adaptation. Sand's historical performance of gender identity thus becomes incorporated into the drama of *Gabriel*.

Works Cited

Andrews, Naomi. *Socialism's Muse: Gender in the Intellectual Landscape of French Romantic Socialism*. Lanham: Lexington, 2006. Print.

Bard, Christine. "Le 'DB58' aux Archives de la Préfecture de Police." *Clio: Histoire, femmes et sociétés* 10 (1999): 2–9. Web. 8 Jan. 2010.

Beauvoir, Simone de. *The Second Sex*. Trans. H. M. Parshley. New York: Random, 1974. Print.

Bergman-Carton, Janis. *The Woman of Ideas in French Art, 1830–1848*. New Haven: Yale UP, 1995. Print.

Berlanstein, Lenard R. "Breeches and Breaches: Cross-dress Theater and the Culture of Gender Ambiguity in Modern France." *Comparative Studies in Society and History* 38.2 (1996): 338–69. Print.

Bertrand-Jennings, Chantal. *Un autre mal du siècle: Le romantisme des romancières, 1800–1846*. Toulouse: PU de Mirail, 2005. Print.

Burton, Jane. *Napoleon and the Woman Question: Discourses of the Other Sex in French Education, Medicine, and Medical Law*. Lubbock: Texas Tech UP, 2007. Print.

Cohen, Margaret. *The Sentimental Education of the Novel*. Princeton: Princeton UP, 1999. Print.

Cohen, Richard. *By the Sword: A History of Gladiators, Musketeers, Samurai, Swashbucklers, and Olympic Champions*. New York: Random, 2002. Print.

Cox, Philip. *Reading Adaptations: Novels and Verse Narratives on the Stage, 1790–1840*. Manchester: Manchester UP, 2000. Print.

Daniels, Barry, ed. *Revolution in the Theater: French Romantic Theories of Drama*. Westport: Greenwood, 1983. Print.

Duvergier, Jean Baptiste. *Collection complète des lois, dècrets, ordonnances, règlemens, avis du Conseil-d'État*. Paris, 1834. *Google Book Search*. Web. 28 Jan. 2010.

Ezdinli, Leyla. *George Sand's Literary Transvestism: Pre-texts and Contexts*. Diss. Princeton U, 1987. Ann Arbor: UMI, 1988. Print.

Fraisse, Geneviève. *Reason's Muse: Sexual Difference and the Birth of Democracy*. Trans. Jane Marie Todd. Chicago: U of Chicago P, 1994. Print.

Freadman, Anne. "Of Cats and Companions, and the Name of George Sand." *Grafts: Feminist Cultural Criticism*. Ed. Susan Sheridan. London: Verso, 1988. 125–56. Print.

Garaguel, Clément. Rev. of *Théâtre complet*, vol. 1, by George Sand. *Journal des débats politiques et littéraires*. 4 Sept. 1876: 1–2. Print.

Garval, Michael. "Visions of the Great Woman Writer: Imagining George Sand through Word and Image." Powell and Malkin 213–24.

Gautier, Théophile. *Mademoiselle de Maupin*. Paris: Gallimard, 1973. Print.

Glasgow, Janis. Preface. *Gabriel*. By George Sand. Paris: Des femmes, 1988. 7–38. Print.

Gleizes, Gilles. *Gabriel(le): Adaptation de Gilles Gleizes d'après Gabriel de George Sand*. Martel: Laquet, 1999. Print.

Harkness, Nigel. "Sand, Lamennais et le féminisme: Le cas des *Lettres à Marcie*." Powell and Malkin 185–92.

Harlan, Elizabeth. *George Sand*. New Haven: Yale UP, 2005. Print.

Hart, Kathleen. *Revolution and Women's Autobiography in Nineteenth-Century France*. Amsterdam: Rodopi, 2004. Print.

Harvey, John Robert. *Men in Black*. Chicago: U of Chicago P, 1996. Print.

H. L. Rev. of *La dernière Aldini: Les Maîtres Mosaïstes*. By George Sand. *Le charivari* 18 May 1838. 1–2. Print.

Hunt, Lynn. "Freedom of Dress in Revolutionary France." *From the Royal to the Republican Body*. Ed. Sara E. Melzer and Kathryn Norberg. Berkeley: U of California P, 1998. 224–49. Print.

Kallberg, Jeffrey. *Chopin at the Boundaries. Sex, History, and Musical Genre*. Cambridge: Harvard UP, 1996. Print.

Kniebiehler, Yvonne. *La femme et les médecins*. Paris: Hachette, 1983. Print.

Laqueur, Thomas. *Making Sex: Body and Gender from the Greeks to Freud*. Cambridge: Harvard UP, 1990. Print.

Manifold, Gay. *George Sand's Theatre Career*. Ann Arbor: UMI Research, 1985. Print.

Massardier-Kenney, Françoise. *Gender in the Fiction of George Sand*. Amsterdam: Rodopi, 2000. Print.

Masson, Catherine. "George Sand's *L'autre*: From 'Auto-adaptation' to Rewriting." *Novel Stages: Drama and the Novel in Nineteenth-Century France*. Ed. Pratima Prasad and Susan McCready. Newark: U of Delaware P, 2007. 111–25. Print.

Moses, Claire. *French Feminism in the Nineteenth Century*. Albany: State U of New York P, 1984. Print.

Naginski, Isabelle Hoog. *George Sand: Writing for Her Life*. New Brunswick: Rutgers UP, 1991. Print.

Nesci, Catherine. *Le flâneur et les flâneuses: Les femmes et la ville à l'époque romantique*. Grenoble: ELLUG, 2007. Print.

Nye, Robert. *Masculinity and Male Codes of Honor in Modern France*. Berkeley: U of California P, 1998. Print.

Offen, Karen. "Le gender est-il une invention américaine?" *Clio: Histoire, femmes et sociétés* 24 (2006): 291–304. Revues.org, 1 Dec. 2008. Web. 14 Aug. 2009.

———. "On the French Origin of the Words *Feminism* and *Feminist*." *Feminist Studies* 8.2 (1988): 45–61. Print.

———. "Reclaiming the European Enlightenment for Feminism; or, Prologemena to Any Future History of Eighteenth-Century Europe." *Perspectives on Feminist Political Thought in European History: From the Middle Ages to the Present*. Ed. Tjitske Akkerman and Siep Sturrman. London: Routledge, 1998. 85–103. Print.

Park, Katharine, and Robert A. Nye, "Destiny Is Anatomy." *New Republic* 18 Feb. 1991: 53–57. Print.

Powell, David. "Entre Mozart et Beethoven: Narrateur, narrataire et narration." *George Sand: Pratiques et imaginaires de l'écriture.* Ed. Brigitte Diaz and Isabelle Hoog Naginski. Caen: PU de Caen, 2006. 311–24. Print.

Powell, David, and Shira Malkin, eds. *Le siècle de George Sand.* Amsterdam: Rodopi, 1998. Print. Faux titre 153.

Prasad, Pratima. "Deceiving Disclosures: Androgyny and George Sand's *Gabriel.*" *French Forum* 24.3 (1999): 331–51. Print.

Rabine, Leslie. "Feminist Writers in French Romanticism." *Studies in Romanticism* 16.4 (1977): 491–507. Print.

Riot-Sarcey, Michèle. *La démocratie à l'épreuve des femmes.* Paris: Albin Michel, 1994. Print.

Rogers, Rebecca. *From the Saloon to the Schoolroom: Educating Bourgeois Girls in Nineteenth-Century France.* University Park: Penn State UP, 2006. Print.

Rossum-Guyon, Françoise van. "À propos d'*Indiana*: La préface de 1832: Problèmes du métadiscours." *George Sand: Colloque de Cérisy, 1981.* Ed. Simone Vierne. Paris: CDU-SEDES, 1983. 71–83. Print.

Sand, George. *Correspondance.* Ed. Georges Lubin. 26 vols. Paris: Garnier, 1964–95. Print.

———. "Essai sur le drame fantastique: Goethe-Byron-Mickiewicz." *Autour de la table.* Paris: Calmann, 1875. 1–18. Print.

———. *Story of My Life.* Ed. Thelma Jurgrau. Albany: State U of New York P, 1991. Print.

———. *Théâtre complet de George Sand.* Paris: Calmann, 1877. Print.

Schor, Naomi. *George Sand and Idealism.* New York: Columbia UP, 1993. Print.

Steinbrügge, Lieselotte. *The Moral Sex: Woman's Nature in the French Enlightenment.* Trans. Pamela F. Selwyn. Oxford: Oxford UP, 1995. Print.

Stolberg, Michael. "A Woman down to her Bones: The Anatomy of Sexual Difference in the Sixteenth and Early Seventeenth Centuries." *Isis* 94.2 (2003): 274–99. Print.

Ubersfeld, Anne. *Reading Theater.* Trans. Frank Collins. Toronto: U of Toronto P, 1999. Print.

Vierne, Simone. *George Sand, la femme qui écrivait la nuit*. Clairmont-Ferrand: PU Blaise Pascal, 2003. Print. Cahiers romantiques.

Waller, Margaret. *The Male Malady: Fictions of Impotence in the French Romantic Novel*. New Brunswick: Rutgers UP, 1993. Print.

Walton, Whitney. *Eve's Proud Descendants: Four Women Writers and Republican Politics in Nineteenth-Century France*. Stanford: Stanford UP, 2000. Print.

SUGGESTIONS FOR FURTHER READING

For a complete, regularly updated list of works by Sand translated into English, as well as information on Sand scholarship and links to other sites on Sand, go to the *George Sand Association* Web site (www.hofstra.edu/georgesand/).

Works on or Relating to *Gabriel*

Bertrand-Jennings, Chantal. *Un autre mal du siècle: Le romantisme des romancières, 1800–1846.* Toulouse: PU du Mirail, 2005. Print.

Frappier-Mazur, Lucienne. "Retraite et ressourcement dans l'imaginaire italien de George Sand: *Lucrezia Floriani, Le Château des Désertes, Elle et Lui.*" *Présences de l'Italie dans l'œuvre de George Sand.* Moncalieri: CIRVI, 2004. 31–43. Print.

Ghillebaert, Françoise. *Disguise in George Sand's Novels.* New York: Lang, 2009. Print.

Hubert-Mathews, Veronica. "*Gabriel* ou la pensée sandienne sur l'identité." *George Sand Studies* 8.1-2 (1994): 19–27. Print.

Laforgue, Pierre. *Corambé: Identité et fiction de soi chez George Sand.* Paris: Klincksieck, 2003. Print.

Manifold, Gay. *George Sand's Gabriel.* Westport: Greenwood, 1992. Print.

Massardier-Kenney, Françoise. *Gender in the Fiction of George Sand*. Amsterdam: Rodopi, 2000. Print.

McCall, Anne. "George Sand and the Genealogy of Terror." *L'Esprit Créateur* 34.4 (1995): 38–48. Print.

Prasad, Pratima. "Deceiving Disclosures: Androgyny and George Sand's *Gabriel*." *French Forum* 24.3 (1999): 331–51. Print.

Androgyny and Transvestism

Bard, Christine. "Le 'DB58' aux Archives de la Préfecture de Police." *Clio: Histoire, femmes et sociétés* 10 (1999): 2–9 Web. 8 Jan. 2010.

Berlanstein, Lenard R. "Breeches and Breaches: Cross-dress Theater and the Culture of Gender Ambiguity in Modern France." *Comparative Studies in Society and History* 38.2 (1996): 338–69. Print.

Bullough, Bonnie, and Vern Bullough. *Cross-Dressing, Sex, and Gender*. Philadelphia: U of Pennsylvania P, 1993. Print.

Dekker, Rudolf M., and Lotte G. van de Pol. *The Tradition of Female Transvestism in Early Modern Europe*. New York: St. Martin's, 1989. Print.

Garber, Marjorie. *Vested Interests: Cross-Dressing and Cultural Anxiety*. New York: Routledge, 1997. Print.

Genevray, Françoise. "Aurore Dupin, épouse Dudevant, alias George Sand: De quelques travestissements sandiens." *Travestissements féminins et liberté(s)*. Ed. Guyonne Leduc. Paris: L'Harmattan, 2006. 253–63. Print.

Monneyron, Frédéric. *L'androgyne romantique: Du mythe au mythe littéraire*. Grenoble: Ellug, 1994. Print.

Reid, Martine. *Signer Sand, l'œuvre et le nom*. Paris: Belin, 2003. Print.

Velay-Vallantin, Catherine. *La fille en garçon*. Carcassone: Garae, 1992. Print.

Vierne, Simone. "Les pantalons de Mme Sand." *Vêtement et littérature.* Ed. F. Monneyron. Perpignan: PU de Perpignan, 2001. 13–38. Print.

The Woman Question in Nineteenth-Century France

Leroux, Pierre, and Jean Reynaud. *Encyclopédie nouvelle.* Ed. Jean-Pierre Lacassagne. Geneva: Slatkine Rpts., 1991. Print.

Moses, Claire Goldberg, and Leslie Rabine. *Feminism, Socialism, and French Romanticism.* Bloomington: Indiana UP, 1993. Print.

Offen, Karen. *European Feminisms, 1700–1950: A Political History.* Stanford: Stanford UP, 2000. Print.

———. "Feminism." *Encyclopedia of Social History.* Ed. Peter N. Stearns. New York: Garland, 1994. 271–72. Print.

George Sand and French Romantic Theater

Frappier-Mazur, Lucienne. "Le monde du théâtre et le rêve communautaire dans les romans de George Sand." *Romanic Review* 96.3-4 (2005): 409–20. Print.

Malkin, Shira. "Between the Bastille and the Madeleine: George Sand's Theater Politics, 1832–1848." *Le siècle de George Sand.* Ed. David Powell and Malkin. Amsterdam: Rodopi, 1998. 73–83. Print. Faux titre 153.

Michelot, Isabelle. "De la théâtralité de l'intime à la théâtralisation du conflit." *George Sand: Une écriture expérimentale.* New Orleans: PU du Nouveau Monde, 2006. 247–58. Print.

NOTE ON THE TRANSLATION

To translate a neglected text is to resurrect a lost world. Our translation was guided by a scrupulous respect for the style, tone, and content of the text as it first appeared in *La revue des deux mondes*, in three installments, on 1 July, 15 July, and 1 August 1839. It thus differs significantly from Gay Manifold's 1992 translation, from which original passages were excised. Though translation is inevitably an interpretive act, we made each verbal choice with a concerted regard for George Sand's complex relation to the aesthetic, linguistic, and social conventions of her time.

Gabriel is a nineteenth-century French drama set in seventeenth-century Italy. For the sake of atmosphere and historical accuracy, we took into account both seventeenth-century and early-nineteenth-century linguistic usage, including the multiple connotations of words that were in a state of transition. The English language shifted more dramatically than the French did during the same time period, and the overall register of *Gabriel* is more modern in French than it would sound in authentic post-Renaissance English. Thus we gave priority to English expressions that were in use during both time periods, and we generally avoided vocabulary belonging exclusively to Early Modern English (roughly, the years between 1500 and 1700). We chose not to translate the informal second-person address in French (*tu*) as its English equivalent (*thou*), preferring instead to translate both the informal and formal second-person pronoun (*vous*) as the more modern-sounding *you*. Notes have been added to the translation to explain where or why different registers are used.

The thematic preoccupation with gender simultaneously required us to evaluate the significance of grammatical gender on a case-by-case basis. The French word *créature*, for instance, is grammatically feminine, but only sometimes does it specifically designate a woman. Thus Astolphe refers to the courtesan Faustina as a "creature," which in certain contexts was once a derogatory term in both French and English meaning "a woman of loose morals." *Creature* could also have a positive connotation for a woman, as in the phrase "charming creature." Sometimes, however, we favored the gender-neutral word *being*, as when we translated the musings of Gabriel's tutor about "the future of this strange being" (*l'avenir de cette étrange créature*). The phrase "strange creature" calls *subhuman* to mind, and in any case textual evidence indicates that the tutor thinks of Gabriel as a man.

Other masculine and feminine markers required careful consideration. In one case, it was necessary to omit the personal pronouns from a line to preserve the ambiguity of the French indirect object pronoun *lui*, which can be masculine or feminine. After provoking a duel to establish the truth of Gabriel's sex, Antonio states in an aside, "At the slightest scratch, the doublet will have to come off." We wished to avoid the awkwardness of the more literal rendering, "If I scratch him or her just a little, the doublet will have to come off" (*Si je lui fais une égratignure, il faudra bien ôter le pourpoint*). On the other hand, we retained the masculine, singular, direct-object pronoun in the preface, where Sand states, "Indeed, the artist needs, by way of some invention, to escape the real world that troubles, oppresses, bores, or grieves him" (*L'artiste a précisément besoin de sortir, par une invention quelconque, du monde positif qui l'inquiète, l'oppresse, l'ennuie, ou le navre*). Sand frequently assumed a male authorial voice in her prefaces.

Because *Gabriel* lends itself to stage adaptation, we sought to maximize each phrase's potential to be spoken aloud effectively for a theatrical performance. To that end, we preferred shorter words to their longer counterparts and occasionally replaced demonstrative pronouns (*this*) with definite articles (*the*). We favored the simple present tense (e.g., *feel*) over the continuous present (*am feeling*) and sought other ways to avoid -*ing* words (*all* instead of *everything*). In some cases, the most exact translation of a passage was abandoned if it contained distracting alliteration not found in the original. Thus Astolphe says, "The wine I drank tonight was dreadful" rather than "I drank a dreadful wine tonight" (*J'ai bu ce soir du vin détestable*). We frequently altered the order of words in a sentence to give it more punch. Gabriel says, "On days when my head burns in the heat of the noonday sun, and my horse and I are both exhilarated from running, I jump over the most terrifying crags of our mountains just for the sheer thrill of it" (*Il y des jours où, sous l'ardent soleil de midi, quand mon front est en feu, quand mon cheval est enivré, comme moi, de la course, je franchirais, seulement pour me divertir, les plus affreux précipices de nos montagnes*). Had we respected the original word order, the sentence would have ended with the comparatively flaccid "crags of our mountains."

Usually, however, we chose not to cut, modernize, or otherwise alter passages merely for the purpose of making them sound less strange or overwrought to a modern audience. Sand's heroine, who takes her name from the angel Gabriel, reads her tragic fate in the ominous swerving of a horse or howling of a dog, as if she and the other characters were connected to invisible forces. When struggling to represent her religious idea of love to the cynical Astolphe, she speaks almost as if she herself were translating from another language: "Your soul has lost the flower of its generous youth. It is weighed down by a hidden remorse that yet fails to prevent further misdeeds. Ah! No doubt love offers a sanctuary we can no longer return to once we have taken a single step outside its boundaries, and the barrier that separated us from harm can no longer be raised up again" (*Ton âme a perdu la fleur de sa jeunesse magnanime; un secret remords la contriste sans la préserver de nouvelles fautes. Ah! sans doute il est dans l'amour un sanctuaire dans lequel on ne peut plus rentrer quand on a fait un seul pas hors de son enceinte, et la barrière qui nous séparait du mal ne peut plus être relevée*). Even in the original French, there is an occasional foreignness to the locutions that is in keeping with the text's radical premise, its unstable generic properties, and otherworldly themes. We wished to recover, not contain, the world of *Gabriel*.

GEORGE SAND

Gabriel

To Albert Grzymala
(Tribute to a faraway brother)

Albert Grzymala (1793–1870), Polish patriot, émigré, and devoted friend of Sand's lover, Frédéric Chopin. Sand uses the word "brother" here to express fondness for Grzymala.

Author's Foreword

I wrote *Gabriel* in Marseilles, just after returning from Spain, as my children played around me in a hotel room. The noise children make is not bothersome. They live in a world of make-believe, where their fancy can wander unhindered by cold reality. Besides, they too belong to the realm of the ideal, owing to the simplicity of their thoughts.

As for *Gabriel*, it belongs to pure fantasy, in both form and subject. Rarely does the fantasy of artists correspond directly to their actual situation. Or at least, it bears no immediate relation to the preoccupations of their external life. Indeed, the artist needs, by way of some invention, to escape the real world that troubles, oppresses, bores, or grieves him. Anyone who does not know that is hardly himself an artist.

George Sand

Nohant, 21 September 1854

Dramatis Personae

Prince Jules de Bramante
Gabriel de Bramante, Prince Jules's grandson
Count Astolphe de Bramante
Antonio
Menrique
Settimia, Astolphe's mother
Faustina
Périnne, a woman who sells secondhand clothing
Tutor of Gabriel (Father Chiavari)
Marc, an elderly servant
Brother Como, a Franciscan friar, Settimia's confessor
Barbe, Settimia's elderly maiden companion
Giglio
A tavern keeper
Bandits, students, *sbirri*,[1] young men, and courtesans

---

[1] A formal and centrally organized police force did not exist in Italy until the late eighteenth century. The Italian *sbirri* (in French, *sbires*) patrolled the streets and known criminal haunts to break up brawls and other illegal gatherings. The name, derived from Latin, refers to the red cloak their captain wore.

PROLOGUE

The castle of Bramante.

Scene 1

The Prince, The Tutor, Marc.

Prince Jules, in traveling clothes, sits in a large armchair.
The Tutor stands before him; Marc serves him wine.

TUTOR: Is Your Highness still tired?

PRINCE: No. Old wine is a friend to old blood. I feel much better now.

TUTOR: What a long and arduous journey Your Highness has made!—and with such speed—

PRINCE: Now that I am fourscore years and upward, it is arduous indeed. I remember a time when it would have required almost no effort. I used to travel across the whole of Italy for a trifle, a dalliance, a whim. Now, only something of utmost importance can induce me to travel half the distance in a litter that I used to cover by horseback . . . Was I not last here ten years ago, Marc?

7

MARC (*visibly intimidated*): Oh! Ay, my lord.

PRINCE: Then, you were still young and vigorous. In fact, you are hardly sixty. That is still young![2]

MARC: Ay, my lord.

PRINCE (*aside to Tutor*): He is still dull-witted, I take it? (*Aloud.*) Go now, my good Marc. Leave the bottle here.

MARC: Oh! Ay, my lord. (*Hesitates to leave.*)

PRINCE (*feigns benevolence*): Go, my friend.

MARC: My lord . . . should I not inform Lord Gabriel that Your Highness is here?[3]

PRINCE (*with anger*): Have I not expressly forbidden you to do so?

TUTOR: You well know that His Highness wishes to surprise Lord Gabriel.

PRINCE: You alone saw me arrive. My people are incapable of indiscretion. If anyone is indiscreet, I shall hold you responsible.

Marc exits, trembling.

---

[2] As was customary, the servant Marc uses *vous* to address his superiors, who address him with *tu*. The people of higher rank, including the tutor, all address one another as *vous*.

[3] The son of a sovereign's son was referred to as "Lord" followed by the given name; members of the nobility were referred to as "Lord" followed by the surname.

Scene 2

Prince, Tutor.

PRINCE: Can that man be trusted?

TUTOR: As myself, my lord.

PRINCE: And . . . he is the only one, besides you and Gabriel's nanny, who has ever known . . .

TUTOR: He, the nanny, and I are the only ones in the world, after Your Highness, with any knowledge of this important secret.

PRINCE: Important! Indeed, a dreadful, frightening secret that gnaws at my soul now and then, almost like guilt. So tell me, Father Chiavari, never the slightest indiscretion . . .

TUTOR: None whatsoever, my lord.

PRINCE: And those who see him every day have never had the faintest doubt?

TUTOR: Never, my lord.

PRINCE: So you were not lying in your letters just to please me? You wrote nothing but the absolute truth?

TUTOR: Your Highness will see for yourself.

PRINCE: That is true! . . . and as the moment draws near, the emotion is quite extraordinary.

TUTOR: Your paternal heart will have cause to rejoice.

PRINCE: My paternal heart! . . . Father, let us leave that expression to those who use it rightly. If such people

9

knew what a brazen, almost insane lie I was forced to concoct for the sake of a peaceful and respectable old age, they would castigate me harshly. That much I know! So let us not borrow their language of common, ordinary tenderness. My feelings for the children of my blood have been more serious and profound.

TUTOR: Passionate feelings!

PRINCE: Do not flatter me. One could just as well call them criminal. I know what words are worth, and I give them no consequence. Above the commonplace duties and trivial cares of ordinary fatherhood are the courageous duties and devouring ambitions of patrician paternity. I have fulfilled them with desperate audacity. May the future not sully my memory and disgrace my proud name over legal squabbles or moral quandaries!

TUTOR: Thus far, fate has splendidly served your plans.

PRINCE (*after a moment of silence*): You wrote that he is handsome?

TUTOR: Admirable! The living image of his father.

PRINCE: I hope he has more vitality!

TUTOR: As I have often written Your Highness, incredible vitality!

PRINCE: His poor father! He was a timid sort . . . with a timorous soul. Good old Julien! With what difficulty I persuaded him to keep this secret from his confessor on his deathbed! No doubt the burden brought on his death more quickly . . .

TUTOR: Or was it rather the grief caused by the premature death of his beautiful young wife . . .

PRINCE: I have already ordered you not to sugar over things, Father Chiavari. I belong to the breed of men who can endure the unmitigated truth. I know I have made hearts bleed, and that another one is soon to do so. No matter, what is done is done . . . He just turned seventeen; he must be rather tall?

TUTOR: He is over five feet tall, my lord, and still growing at a fast pace.[4]

PRINCE (*visibly overjoyed*): In truth! Fate is certainly helping us! And what about his face, is it already a little masculine? Already! I would even fool myself . . . No, tell me no more, I shall see soon enough . . . Tell me only about his mind, his education.

TUTOR: All was carried out exactly as Your Highness ordered, and with miraculous success.

PRINCE: Fate be praised! . . . assuming you do not exaggerate, Father Chiavari. So every effort was made to mold his mind and endow him with all the knowledge a prince must possess to be worthy of his name and rank?

TUTOR: Your Highness is a vastly learned man. You yourself will be able to examine my noble pupil and see that his studies have been thorough and truly manly.

PRINCE: Latin and Greek, I hope?

---

[4] At the time, five feet was an above-average height for women.

TUTOR: He knows Latin as well as you, I daresay, my lord, and Greek . . . like . . . *(Smiles broadly.)*

PRINCE *(laughs indulgently)*: Like you, Father Chiavari? Wonderful. I thank you and acknowledge your superior skills in the subject. Now what about history, philosophy, literature?

TUTOR: I can assure you of that. All the honor goes to the pupil's exceptional intelligence. His progress has been prodigiously rapid.

PRINCE: He enjoys learning? And serious pursuits?

TUTOR: He enjoys learning, and also vigorous exercise—hunting, fencing, running. His skill, perseverance, and courage add to his physical strength. He enjoys serious pursuits, but also what everyone likes at his age: beautiful horses, fine clothes, weapons that sparkle and gleam.

PRINCE: If that is the case, then so much the better, and you have perfectly understood my intentions. Now, one more thing. Have you been able to impart to him that particular, peculiar disposition . . . Do you know what I am getting at?

TUTOR: Ay, my lord. From his earliest childhood (Your Highness himself gave Gabriel's imagination this initial disposition), he has been imbued with the grandeur of man's role and the lowliness of woman's in nature and society. The very first paintings that caught his eye, the very first historical facts that awakened his thoughts, showed him the weakness and subjection of the one sex and the freedom and power of the other.) You can see on these panels the frescoes that you ordered me to have painted: here, the abduction of the Sabine women; on this other one, the treason of Tarpeia. Then the crime and punishment of the Danaids.[5] There, you have the sale of women slaves in the Orient; over there, repudiated queens, spurned or betrayed mistresses, Hindu widows

---

[5] Classical sources indicate that the Sabine story was set in the eighth century BC. Because the newly formed Roman state had a shortage of women, Romulus ordered a celebration that attracted many people of other countries, including the Sabines. Once the show was under way, the young Roman men, according to a plan, forcibly carried off the young Sabine women. Mythological abduction scenes in works of art helped bolster the authoritarian rule of sovereigns during the sixteenth and seventeenth centuries; in Italy, panels and other domestic furnishings featuring the Sabine story were often wedding gifts that helped reinforce the bride's submissive and child-bearing role (Musacchio). Italy, a favorite travel destination for Sand, was the setting for many of her novels. She traveled there for the first time at the end of 1833, remaining until August 1834. That she knew Italian art is evidenced by her novel about Renaissance Italian artists, *Les maîtres mosaïstes* (*The Master Mosaic Makers*). She was thus well acquainted with the sorts of panels and frescoes one would expect to find in the homes of the ancient Italian aristocracy (see *Présences*: Poli; Rouget).

Tarpeia was the daughter of Tarpeius, the commander of the Capitoline fortress at Rome. A war between the Romans and Sabines had been provoked by the abduction of the Sabine women. Tarpeia let the Sabines into her father's fortress after making them promise to give her what they wore on their left arms (their shields, according to one tradition; their bracelets, according to another). When Tarpeia opened the city gates, the Sabines killed her. Her name became synonymous with treachery.

The fifty Danaids, who were the daughters of Danaus, lived in Egypt. To avoid being married to their first cousins, they fled to Argos. Their cousins pursued them and forced them to accept them as their husbands. But on the wedding night, all but one of the Danaid women killed their bridegrooms. Their punishment is said to be forever trying to carry water from one place to another in a sieve.

13

sacrificed on their husbands' funeral pyres. Everywhere you see woman as slave, property, conquest, trying to free herself from her fetters only to undergo worse punishment, and able to break away only through lies, betrayal, and futile, cowardly crimes.

PRINCE: And what sentiments have these ever-present examples inspired in him?

TUTOR: A mixture of horror and compassion, sympathy and hatred . . .

PRINCE: Sympathy, you say? Has he ever seen a woman? Was he ever in a position to exchange words with persons of the other sex?

TUTOR: Some words, perhaps, but ideas never. He has seen country girls only from afar, and he feels an insuperable repugnance to speak to them.

PRINCE: And deep down you are quite sure he has no idea of the truth?

TUTOR: His upbringing has been so chaste, his thoughts are so pure, and his innocence has shrouded the truth in such an impenetrable veil, that he suspects nothing, and will learn only from the words of Your Highness what he must now learn. But I must warn you that it will be a severe blow, a terribly painful experience, perhaps traumatic . . . Given the circumstances, it is only to be expected . . .

PRINCE: Quite so . . . good. You will prepare him with a few words as we agreed.

TUTOR: My lord, I hear a horse galloping . . . There he is. If you wish to see him through this window . . . , he approaches.

PRINCE (*rises eagerly and looks out the window while hidden by the curtain*): What! That young man on a black horse quick as lightning?

TUTOR (*proudly*): Ay, my lord.

PRINCE: The dust he raises conceals his features . . . What a beautiful head of hair, and elegant build . . . Yes, he must be a handsome cavalier . . . well-seated on his horse, graceful, skilled, strong even . . . What? Is he going to jump over the fence, the young fool?

TUTOR: He always does, my lord.

PRINCE: Bravissimo! I could not have done better myself at twenty-five. Father, if the rest of his education has been as successful, then I compliment you and will reward you to your satisfaction, rest assured. I now retire to the room you have arranged for me. Behind that partition, I shall hear you talk to him. I must prepare myself to see him, and know him a little before he hears me. I admit to being rather nervous, Father Chiavari. This is a solemn moment for me and for this child. Everything will be determined very shortly. The honor of an entire family depends upon the way he first reacts. Honor! such an empty word, and yet so powerful!

TUTOR: Victory will be yours as always, my lord. His romantic soul, whose tendencies I could not mold exactly as you wished, will perhaps revolt when the truth hits him. But the horror of enslavement, and the thirst for independence, action, and glory will triumph over all his scruples.

PRINCE: May you be right! I hear him . . . his step is firm . . . I shall go in here . . . I give you an hour . . . more or less, according to—

TUTOR: My lord, you will hear everything. When you wish him to appear before you, knock over a piece of furniture and I will understand.

PRINCE: Very well! (*Enters the adjoining room.*)

Scene 3

Tutor, Gabriel.

Gabriel is in fashionable hunting attire; has long, disheveled, curly hair; and holds a riding crop. He throws himself into a chair, out of breath, and wipes his brow.

GABRIEL: Whew! I am exhausted.

TUTOR: Indeed you look pale, sir. Have you had a mishap?

GABRIEL: No, but my horse almost threw me. On three different occasions, he swerved in the middle of a run. It is strange; it never happened before with this horse. My groom says it is a bad omen. I would say it is an omen that my horse is becoming skittish.

TUTOR: You seem distraught . . . You say you were almost thrown?

GABRIEL: Yes, I actually came close the third time, and for a moment I was frightened.

TUTOR: You, such a good rider, frightened?

GABRIEL: Well, I had a scare if you prefer.

TUTOR: Do lower your voice, sir, someone might hear you.

GABRIEL: What matter? Do I ever curb my language or disguise my thoughts? What is there to be ashamed of?

TUTOR: A man must never be afraid.

GABRIEL: My dear Father Chiavari, it is the same as saying that a man must never feel cold or never fall ill. I only believe that a man should never let his enemy see when he is afraid.

TUTOR: Man has a natural disposition to confront danger, and that in particular is what distinguishes him from woman.

GABRIEL: Oh, women, women! I do not know why you are always talking to me about women. Personally, I do not feel that my soul has a sex, as you so often try to convince me. I do not feel within myself an absolute faculty for anything whatsoever. For instance, I do not feel absolutely brave or absolutely cowardly. On days when my head burns in the heat of the noonday sun, and my horse and I are both exhilarated from running, I jump over the most terrifying crags of our mountains just for the sheer thrill of it. On nights when a window rattles in the wind, and the noise makes me shiver, I would not for all the glories of the world cross the threshold of the chapel without a lamp. Believe me, we are all under the impression of the moment. Any man who boasted to me of not knowing fear would strike me as a huge braggart, just as a woman who told me she felt brave on some days would not surprise me. When I was still a child, I often exposed myself to danger more willingly than today, simply because I was not aware of any danger.

TUTOR: My dear Gabriel, you are very contentious today. But let us drop the matter. I have to talk to you about—

GABRIEL: No, no! I want to finish my point and dispute your line of reasoning . . . I know very well why you wish to change the subject . . .

TUTOR: I do not understand you.

GABRIEL: Indeed yes! Do you remember that stream you did not wish to cross because the frail wooden footbridge barely held together anymore? And yet, I was already halfway across! You would not leave the bank, and I had to come back at your insistence. Were you not afraid then?

TUTOR: I do not remember that.

GABRIEL: Oh, yes you do!

TUTOR: I must have been afraid for you.

GABRIEL: No, because I was already halfway across. It was as dangerous for me to come back as to continue.

TUTOR: And your point is . . .

GABRIEL: That since I was ten years old and unaware of danger, I was bolder than you, a wise and cautious man. Which proves that absolute bravery is not found exclusively in men but also in children and, who knows, perhaps in women.

TUTOR: Where did you get these notions? I have never seen you so argumentative.

GABRIEL: Oh, well! I do not tell you everything that goes on in my head.

TUTOR (*uneasy*): What, for instance?

GABRIEL: Bah! Just things! I am in a strange mood today. I feel like poking fun at everything.

TUTOR: And who has made you so lighthearted?

GABRIEL: On the contrary, I am sad. Of all things, I had a strange dream last night that has preoccupied and somewhat haunted me all day.

TUTOR: What childishness! And this dream—

GABRIEL: I dreamed I was a woman.

TUTOR: That is peculiar indeed . . . And from where did you get this imaginary idea?

GABRIEL: Where do dreams come from? That would be for you to explain to me, dear teacher.

TUTOR: I assume you found the dream unpleasant?

GABRIEL: Not in the least, because in my dream I was not earthbound. I had wings, and was flying upward through other worlds, toward some kind of ideal world. Sublime voices sang all around me, and though I could see no one, my face was reflected in the airy, shining clouds passing through the ether. I was a young girl dressed in a long flowing gown and crowned with flowers. ·

TUTOR: Then you were an angel, not a woman.

GABRIEL: I was a woman. For suddenly my wings grew numb, the ether closed about my head like an impenetrable crystal vault, and I was falling, falling . . . and around my neck hung a heavy chain whose weight pulled me toward the abyss. Then I awoke, overcome with sadness, weariness, and fright . . . Oh well, let us drop the matter. What have you to teach me today?

TUTOR: We must have a serious conversation. I have important news to tell you, and I need your undivided attention.

GABRIEL: News! It will be the first I have ever had, because I have always heard the same things since I was born. Is it a letter from my grandfather?

TUTOR: Better than that.

GABRIEL: A present? What do I care? I am not a child anymore who gets excited about a new weapon or garment. I cannot understand why my grandfather thinks only of clothing or pastimes when it comes to me.

TUTOR: But you enjoy adornment, perhaps a little too much.

GABRIEL: True, but I wish my grandfather would consider me a young man and grant me the signal favor of making his acquaintance.

TUTOR: Very well, my dear sir, you will soon have that honor.

GABRIEL: I am told so every year.

TUTOR: Tomorrow will be the day.

GABRIEL (*genuinely pleased*): Aha! Finally!

TUTOR: Does the news fulfill all your wishes?

GABRIEL: Yes, I have much to tell my noble relative, many questions to ask him, and probably reproaches to make.

TUTOR (*startled*): Reproaches?

GABRIEL: Yes, for keeping me isolated all my life. I am tired of it. I long to know this world everyone talks about, these men I have heard praised, and these women I have heard debased, the wealth people value, and the pleasures everyone seeks . . . I long to know, feel, possess, brave everything! Oh! That surprises you, but listen: you can raise falcons in a cage and make them lose the memory or instinct of freedom. But a young man is a bird endowed with more memory and reflection.

TUTOR: Your illustrious relative will make his intentions known to you, and you will convey your wishes to him. My work with you is done, my dear pupil. But I do not want His Highness to think I did a bad job.

GABRIEL: Many thanks! If I show some good sense, all the credit will go to my dear tutor. And if my grandfather finds me a fool, then my tutor will wash his hands of it by saying he could get nothing into my poor head.

TUTOR: You imp! Are you ever going to listen to me?

GABRIEL: What is it? I thought you had told me everything.

TUTOR: I have not begun.

GABRIEL: Will it take very long?

TUTOR: Not unless you repeatedly interrupt me.

GABRIEL: I will hold my tongue.

TUTOR: I have often explained to you what it means to come of age, and how the succession of a principality with its titles, rights, privileges, honors, and riches attached . . . (*Gabriel conceals a yawn.*) Are you listening?

GABRIEL: Pardon me.

TUTOR: As I was saying . . .

GABRIEL: Oh! for the love of God, Father, do not start over. I can finish the sentence, I know it by heart: ". . . and riches attached, can pass alternatively in the family from the older branch to the younger, and pass back again, reciprocally, by the law which transmits the inheritance to the oldest of the male children of one of the branches, when the collateral branch finds itself represented by only female children." Is that all you had new and interesting to tell me? Truly, had you not taught me worthier things than that, I would just as soon know nothing at all.

TUTOR: Have a little patience, and recall how often you require me to do the same with you.

GABRIEL: That is true, my friend, pardon me. I am out of sorts today.

TUTOR: I can tell. It might be better to resume our conversation tomorrow or this evening.

Slight noise in the adjoining room.

GABRIEL: Who is in there?

TUTOR: Listen to me, and you will find out.

GABRIEL (*with feeling*): Is it he? Could it be my grandfather?

TUTOR: Maybe.

GABRIEL (*runs to the door*): What do you mean, maybe? And you keep me waiting! . . . (*Tries to open the door, but it is locked from the inside.*) What! He is here but kept hidden from me!

TUTOR: Stop, he is resting.

GABRIEL: No! He just stirred; he made a noise.

TUTOR: He is tired and ill. You may not see him.

GABRIEL: Why has he locked me out? I would have gone in without making noise. I would have watched over him lovingly while he slept and contemplated his venerable features. Listen, Father Chiavari, I have always felt that he does not love me. I am alone in the world. I have only one protector, one relative, and he does not know me, does not love me!

TUTOR: My dear pupil, you must banish from your mind such sad and shameful thoughts! Your illustrious grandparent did not show you those banal signs of affection displayed by commoners . . .

GABRIEL: Would to God I had been born a commoner! I would not be unknown, a stranger to the head of my family.

TUTOR: Gabriel, today you will learn a great secret, and everything that has seemed enigmatic to you until now will be explained. I may as well tell you, the most solemn, the most formidable hour is about to arrive for you. You will see what immeasurable, what unbelievable solicitude you have received from the moment of your birth until now. Steel yourself. You have a great resolution to make, a great destiny to accept today. When you have learned what you did not know, you will not claim to be unloved. You at least know that your birth was awaited like a celestial favor, like a miracle. Your father was ill, and there was almost no hope of seeing him bring forth an heir to his title and riches. The younger branch of the Bramante family was already gloating in hopes of succeeding to the glorious title you will hold one day . . .

GABRIEL: Oh! I know all that. Besides, I have figured out many things you never told me. It must have been jealousy that divided the two brothers, Julien my father and Octave my uncle. And perhaps my grandfather harbored in his soul a secret preference for his elder son . . . Then I came into the world. Great joy for everyone, except me. I was not endowed by heaven with a character equal to these grave circumstances.

TUTOR: What are you saying?

GABRIEL: I am saying that the transmission of inheritance solely from male to male is a troublesome law, perhaps even unjust. The continual movement of property from one to the other branch of the family cannot help but stir up jealousy, sharpen resentments, incite hatred between close relatives, force fathers to hate their daughters, and make mothers blush to have brought forth children of their own sex . . . What can I say! Ambition and greed must run deep in a family gathered like a pack of starving dogs around the quarry of the elder son. And history has taught me that the result can be horrible crimes that put humanity to shame. So why do you stare at me like that, my dear master, looking confused? Did you not bring me up on stories of heroes and cowards? Have you not always called my attention to the conflict between heroic honesty and base deceit? Does it surprise you that I would retain from all that some notion of justice, some love for the truth?

TUTOR (*lowers his voice*): You are right, Gabriel, but for heaven's sake, try to be less defiant and outspoken in the presence of your grandfather.

Impatient movement in the adjoining room.

GABRIEL (*in a loud voice*): Listen, Father, I have a better opinion of my grandfather. I wish he could hear me. Maybe his presence will intimidate me, but I would be greatly relieved if he were able to look into my soul and realize he was wrong to send me only children's toys these past two years.

TUTOR: I repeat, you cannot imagine what fondness he has had for you. Do not be ungrateful to heaven. You could have been born without all the wealth that fortune has bestowed upon you, without all the loving care that has been secretly and steadily lavished on you.

GABRIEL: No doubt I could have been born a woman, and then good-bye to fortune and family love! I would have been a cursed creature, and by now I would no doubt be hidden away in some convent expiating the crime of my birth. But it is not my grandfather who did me the great honor of making me belong to the male race.

TUTOR (*increasingly dismayed*): Gabriel, you do not know what you are saying.

GABRIEL: How charming if I had my grandfather to thank for being born his grandson! He is the one who

26

should thank me for being born just as he wanted, since he hated . . . or at least did not love his son Octave. He would have been mortified to leave his title to Octave's children. Oh! I understood that a long time ago in spite of you. You are not a great diplomat, my good priest; you are too honest for that . . .

TUTOR (*in a low voice*): Gabriel, I beseech you . . .

A piece of furniture falls noisily in the adjoining room.

GABRIEL: Well, now the prince is awake for sure. I am going to see him at last. I shall learn his intentions; I am going in there. (*Goes resolutely to the door.*)

The Prince opens it for him and appears on the threshold. Gabriel halts, cowed. The Prince takes his hand and leads him into the adjoining room, slamming the door behind him.

Scene 4

TUTOR (*alone*): The old man is angry, the child rebellious, and I am at an utter loss. Old Jules can be vindictive, and vengeance is so easy for men in power! But his bizarre moods and unpredictable decisions might make him suddenly value what he regards now as my mistake. Besides, he is above all a shrewd man, and though he cares not for justice, he is discerning. He will

comprehend that the fault is all his and that his outlandish scheme could only have outlandish results. But what
raging wasp has stung my pupil's tongue today? Never
before have I seen him like this. As to the future of this
strange being, I could speculate endlessly but in vain: his
future is elusive, like the nature of his mind . . . Was I to
be a magician who could outwit nature and thwart the
divine purpose in a human brain? Perhaps I could have,
by resorting to lies and corruption. But as the child said,
I was too honest to carry out the difficult task assigned
to me. I was unable to hide from him that true morality
can exist. What was intended to warp his judgment has
only served to guide it . . . (*Listens to the voices that can be
heard in the adjoining room.*) They have raised their voices
. . . the old man sounds dry and bitter. The child shakes
with anger . . . What! He dares stand up to a man no one
stands up to with impunity! Dear God! Please do not let
Gabriel become an object of that pitiless man's hatred!
(*Listens again.*) The old man threatens, the child resists
. . . This child is noble and generous, yes, he is a noble
soul. It would have been better to corrupt and deprave
him, because his need for justice and truth will torture
him in the impossible situation he is being thrown into.
Alas! ambition, you torment of princes, what infamous
advice you give them, and what consolation you can offer
at the same time! . . . Yes, ambition, vanity, can prevail in

Gabriel's soul and arm him against despair. (*Listens.*) The Prince is vehement . . . he is coming in here . . . Should I face his wrath? Yes, for Gabriel's sake. Oh God, let him be angry only with me . . . The storm seems to abate. Now it is Gabriel who speaks with assurance . . . Gabriel! strange and unfortunate creature, unique on this earth . . . my handiwork, which is to say, my pride and remorse! . . . and my agony, too! . . . Oh God! you alone know what torments I have endured for two years . . . Senseless old man! you who never felt your heart beat for anything but false glory, vile and chimerical; you have not the slightest notion of what I have suffered. God, you have given me great strength. I am grateful to you that my trial is over. Will you punish me for having accepted it? No! For someone else in my position might have shamefully abused it . . . and at least I did all I could to protect the being whom I could not save.

Scene 5

Prince, Gabriel, Tutor.

GABRIEL (*incensed*): Leave me alone. I have heard enough. Not another word, or I shall kill myself. Yes, that is the punishment I should inflict on you in order to ruin the mad hopes of your insatiable hatred and outrageous pride.

TUTOR: My dear child, in the name of heaven, control yourself . . . Remember to whom you speak.

GABRIEL: I speak to the one whose slave and victim I am for the rest of my life! Oh, shame! Shame and curses on the day I was born!

PRINCE: Do the pleasures of the flesh already speak to your senses so much that the idea of eternal chastity makes you so upset?

GABRIEL: Quiet, old man! Your lips will shrivel from uttering words whose august and sacred meaning you fail to understand. Do not impute thoughts to me that have never sullied my soul. You have already outraged me enough by making me the instrument of hatred, the accomplice of imposture and fraud from the moment I was born. Must I live under the weight of an eternal lie, a theft the law would punish by imposing the worst of infamies?

TUTOR: Gabriel! Gabriel! You speak to your grand-father! . . .

PRINCE: Let him vent his gall and give full rein to his furor. I cannot be bothered with such ravings. I only have one more thing to say to you, Gabriel: you must choose between the brilliant destiny of a prince and the eternal captivity of the cloister! You are still free. You can make my enemies triumph, abase the name you carry, sully the memory of those who brought you into the world, dishonor my white hair . . . If such is your will, just remember that you will be the first to suffer infamy and poverty. Then you will see if satisfying your crudest instincts can make up for the horror of such ruin.

GABRIEL: Enough, enough, I tell you! The reasons you give for my unhappiness reflect only your own base way of thinking, not mine . . . (*Sits down and holds his head in his hands.*)

TUTOR (*in a low voice to the Prince*): My lord, we ought to leave him alone for a while; he is not himself right now.

PRINCE (*also in a low voice*): You are right. Come with me, Father.

TUTOR (*still in a low voice*): Is Your Highness angry with me?

PRINCE (*also in a low voice*): Quite the contrary. You have achieved the goal better than I could have done myself. His character offers more guarantee of discretion than I could ever have dared hope for.

TUTOR (*aside*): Heart of stone!

They exit.

Scene 6

GABRIEL (*alone*): So that *was* the horrible secret I had guessed! At last they dared reveal it to me in person! Impudent old man! You should have writhed in shame when you saw me acting so innocent and shocked (which I only did in order to punish and mislead you)! The fools! How could they believe I was still the dupe of their insolent hoax? An admirable ruse, indeed! To inspire in me the horror of women, only to throw it in my face and say: But this is what you are . . . this is what we will condemn you to if you do not agree to be our accomplice! And my tutor, Father Chiavari himself, whom I took to be so honest and straightforward, he knew! Maybe Marc knows too! How many others might know? I dare not look anyone in the face anymore. Ah! Sometimes I still wanted to doubt it. Oh, my dream! My dream of last night, my wings . . . my chain! (*Weeps bitterly, then wipes his eyes.*) But the old cheat is caught in his own trap. He has exposed to me the weakest spot of his hate-filled heart. Oh, you impostors, I shall punish you! I shall make you suffer with me, make you worry, lose sleep, and fear shame . . . I shall dangle the punishment within a hair's breadth of your white head, old Jules, until your last gasp. You carefully hid from me this young man's existence! Now I shall find solace by repairing the inequity to which I have been made an accomplice! Poor relative, poor victim, like me! Wandering, roving, debt-ridden, sunk in debauchery, they say, debased, depraved, and, alas, perhaps beyond hope. Poverty degrades people brought up to expect honors and to thirst for riches. And the cruel old man rejoices over it! He gloats to see his grandson living in abjection, just because the unfortunate man's father dared defy his iron will, or perhaps expose some of his depravity! Well then! I extend my hand to you, cousin, I who deep down am more debased and unfortunate than you. I shall do my best to save you from the quagmire and purify your soul with a sacred friendship. And if I do not succeed, my wealth will at least deliver you from the abyss of poverty, as I return to you the inheritance that is rightfully yours. And if I cannot restore to you this vain title that you perhaps wish for, and that I blush to bear in your place, I shall do my very best to secure for you the favors of kings that all men vie for. But what is his name? And where is he? I shall find out. I too can dissemble and deceive. And when equality between the two of us has been restored through trust and friendship, then they will learn of it! . . . Then their worry will be most touching. Since you insult me, old Jules!, since you believe chastity is so hard for me, your punishment will be not to realize just how much my soul is more chaste and my will more firm than you can imagine . . . Forward! Courage! My God, my God! You are the father of the orphan, the champion of the weak, the defender of the oppressed!

ACT 1

Scene 1

A tavern. Gabriel, Marc.

Groups seated at other tables; the Tavern Keeper coming and going; then Count Astolphe enters.

GABRIEL (*sits down at a table*): Marc! Have a seat . . . across from me. Sit down now!

MARC (*hesitates to sit*): My lord . . . here? . . .

GABRIEL: Quickly! All those imbeciles are looking at us. Do not be so stiff . . . We are not in my grandfather's castle. Order some wine.

Marc knocks on the table. The Tavern Keeper approaches.

TAVERN KEEPER: What wine shall I serve your excellencies?

MARC (*to Gabriel*): What will be the wine, excellency?

GABRIEL (*to the Tavern Keeper*): Good question! By God! Give us your best. (*The Tavern Keeper departs. To Marc.*)

Come now! Could you not adopt a more casual manner? Do you forget where we are, do you want to give away my disguise?

MARC: I will do my best . . . But in truth, I am not accustomed to this . . . Are you quite sure this is the place?

GABRIEL: Very sure . . . Oh, it looks bad, I admit, but it all depends on how you look at things. Come now, old friend, show some confidence.

MARC: It pains me to see you here! . . . If someone were to recognize you . . .

GABRIEL: Well, then! What could make a better effect?

FIRST STUDENT of the group of students: What do you want to bet that worthless young rascal is here with his uncle to get him drunk and then confess his debts between drinks?[6]

SECOND STUDENT: That one? No, he is a proper lad. Just from the look of his mug, you can tell he is a prig.

THIRD STUDENT: Which one?

SECOND STUDENT: The both of them.

MARC (*strikes the table*): Well then, where is that wine?

---

[6] In this scene, the students use *tu* with one another, as befitting young people, especially if they are commoners. The cutthroats use *tu* with one another, and because they come from the dregs of society and wish to insult the victims of their attack, they also use *tu* with Gabriel and Astolphe. Bands of criminals (in Italian, *banditi*) were common in post-Renaissance Italy, which lacked a centrally organized police force.

GABRIEL: Marvelous! Knock louder.

FIRST CUTTHROAT of the band of cutthroats: Some hurry those fellows are in! Is the old fool's throat burning?

SECOND CUTTHROAT: They are well dressed.

THIRD CUTTHROAT: Hm! An old man and a child! What time is it?

FIRST CUTTHROAT: Keep the host busy so that he does not serve them too quickly. By the time they empty two bottles, it will be midnight.

SECOND CUTTHROAT: They are well armed.

THIRD CUTTHROAT: Bah! One has no beard; the other has no teeth.

Astolphe enters.

FIRST CUTTHROAT: Phew! That swashbuckler Astolphe is here. When will we be rid of him?

FOURTH CUTTHROAT: Whenever we like.

SECOND CUTTHROAT: He is alone tonight.

FOURTH CUTTHROAT: Wait, look! (*Indicates the students, who are getting up.*)

FIRST STUDENT: Look, Astolphe is here, the king of carousers. Let us invite him to empty a flask with us. His merrymaking will liven us up.

SECOND STUDENT: Good lord, no. It is getting late; the streets are quite dangerous.

FIRST STUDENT: Do you not have your sword?

SECOND STUDENT: Oh, I am tired of all that foolishness. It is the *sbirri's* job, not ours, to fight with thieves every night.

THIRD STUDENT: And I can hardly put up with your Astolphe. For all that he is a rogue and a degenerate, he can never forget he is a gentleman by birth. Every so often he puts on the airs of a lord, as if he cannot help it. It makes me want to slap him.

SECOND STUDENT: And those two priggish pedants drinking sadly over there in a corner look to me like poorly disguised German barons.

FIRST STUDENT: The company tonight is definitely no good. Let us leave.

They pay the Tavern Keeper and exit. The cutthroats follow all their movements. Gabriel watches Astolphe, who has thrown himself onto a bench with a ferocious air, elbows on the table, neither asking for a drink nor looking at anyone.

MARC (*low, to Gabriel*): He is a handsome young man, but how shabby he appears! Look, his collar is torn and his doublet stained.

GABRIEL: His valet is to blame. What a noble forehead! Ah! If only I had such masculine features and large hands! . . .

FIRST CUTTHROAT (*looks out the window*): They have gone . . . Now if only those two simpletons sitting there with their cups still full would leave, too . . .

SECOND CUTTHROAT: Should we fight him here? The host is a coward.

THIRD CUTTHROAT: All the more reason.

SECOND CUTTHROAT: He will shout.

FOURTH CUTTHROAT: We will quiet him.

The midnight bells ring. Astolphe strikes the table with his fist. The cutthroats watch Gabriel and Astolphe alternately. Gabriel watches only Astolphe.

MARC (*low, to Gabriel*): Some rough men over there keep looking at you.

GABRIEL: They are amused by the clumsy way you hold your glass.

MARC (*drinks*): This wine is terrible, and I fear it is giving me a headache.

Long silence.

FIRST CUTTHROAT: The old man is nodding off.

SECOND CUTTHROAT: He is not drunk.

THIRD CUTTHROAT: But he has seen more than a few winters go by. Go check if Mezzani is somewhere in the street. Now is the moment. That young fellow over there with his big wide eyes has a black velvet overcoat, and that does not mean empty pockets.

Second Cutthroat goes to the door.

TAVERN KEEPER (*to Astolphe*): So, Lord Astolphe, what wine do I have the honor of serving you?

ASTOLPHE: You can go to the devil!

THIRD CUTTHROAT (*to the Tavern Keeper in a lower voice, so Astolphe does not hear*): That lord asked you three times for some malmsey.[7]

TAVERN KEEPER: Is that so? (*Runs out.*)

First Cutthroat gestures to Third Cutthroat, who puts a bench across the door as if by chance. Second Cutthroat enters with a new companion.

FIRST CUTTHROAT: Mezzani?

MEZZANI (*in a low voice*): Got it. Two birds with one stone . . . The timing is good. The night watch just went by. I shall start the fight. (*Astolphe yawns. Loudly.*) What kind of ill-bred boor yawns like that?

ASTOLPHE: You are the only boor here, milord.[8] (*Resumes yawning, stretches his arms with exaggeration.*)

---

[7] Eager to win the tavern keeper's cooperation, the cutthroat respectfully addresses him with *vous*.

[8] Underscoring the irony of addressing him as "milord," Astolphe uses the formal *vous*, though he uses *tu* throughout the rest of the scene when addressing the cutthroats.

MEZZANI: My shabby lord, watch your manners!

ASTOLPHE (*stretches as if to go to sleep*): Hush, ruffian; I need sleep.

FIRST CUTTHROAT (*throws his glass at him*): To your health, Astolphe!

ASTOLPHE: Fine, I was in the mood all day to thrash some blockhead or beat some dog. (*Lunges toward them, shoving his table forward, overturns the cutthroats' table covered with torches and bottles.*)

The fight begins.

MEZZANI (*takes Astolphe by the throat*): Hey! Come on, you oafs, get the youngster.

FIRST CUTTHROAT (*runs to Gabriel*): He is shaking.

Marc lunges but is knocked down. Gabriel kills the Cutthroat at close range with his pistol. Another lunges at him. Marc gets up. They fight. Gabriel is quiet and pale but fights with assurance.

ASTOLPHE (*has freed himself from Mezzani, approaches Gabriel while continuing to fight*): Well done, my young lion! Keep going, my handsome young man! . . . (*Runs Mezzani through with his sword.*)

MEZZANI (*falls*): Help me, comrades! I am dead . . .

TAVERN KEEPER (*cries to the outdoors*): Help! Murder! They slaughter each other in my tavern!

The fight continues.

SECOND CUTTHROAT: Mezzani down. Sancho dying . . . three against three . . . Good night! (*Flees to the door.*)

The other two try to do the same, but Astolphe blocks the way.

ASTOLPHE: Not so hasty. Death to you vile beasts! This is for you, noble butcher! and for you, pickpocket! . . . (*Forces the two into a corner, wounds one who begs for mercy.*)

Marc pursues the other, who tries to flee. Gabriel disarms Third Cutthroat and puts the blade to his throat.

THIRD CUTTHROAT (*to Gabriel*): Mercy, my young master, have mercy! Look, the window is open, I can run away . . . Do not kill me! It was my first crime; it will be my last . . . Do not make me lose faith in God's compassion! Let me go! . . . Have pity on me! . . .

GABRIEL: You wretch! May God hear you and punish you doubly if indeed you blaspheme! . . . Go!

THIRD CUTTHROAT (*jumps out the window*): My name is Giglio . . . I owe you my life! . . . (*Leaps through the window and disappears.*)

The sbirri enter and grab the other two, who are trying to flee.

ASTOLPHE: Good! They are all yours, gentlemen of the law! As usual, you arrive just when you are no longer needed! Get rid of these two corpses for us. (*To Tavern Keeper.*) And you, put the tables back. (*To Gabriel, who is hastily wiping his hands.*) Do not be so dainty, those bloodstains are to your glory, my brave young man!

GABRIEL (*very pale and close to fainting*): Blood horrifies me.

ASTOLPHE: God! No one could tell from the way you fight! Let me shake the little white hand of one who fights like Achilles.

GABRIEL (*wipes his hands with a richly embroidered silk handkerchief*): With all my heart, Lord Astolphe, the most daring of men! (*Shakes his hand.*)

MARC (*to Gabriel*): My lord, are you wounded?

ASTOLPHE: My lord? Indeed, you do look like a prince. Well, since you know my name, you know I am of good family and can count me among your friends without demeaning yourself. (*To the* sbirri, *who have been questioning the Tavern Keeper and now approach Astolphe to arrest him.*) Well, my dear night owls, whom are you after now?

SBIRRI CAPTAIN: Lord Astolphe, you will have to wait in prison until the courts have cleared up the case. (*To Gabriel.*) Sir, you must come along with us too.

ASTOLPHE (*laughs*): What? Cleared it up? It is already clear to me. Murderers attack us, they were five against three, because they counted on the weakness of an old man and a boy . . . But these are brave companions . . . This young man . . . Why, you should get down on your knees, *sbirro*. Meanwhile, take this and have a drink . . . Leave us be . . . (*Rummages in his pockets.*) Ah! I forgot I spent my last coin tonight . . . But tomorrow . . . if I find you again in some den of cutthroats like this, I shall pay you double . . . Agreed? The gentleman here is a prince . . . the prince of . . . the nephew of the cardinal of . . . (*into the* sbirro's *ear*) the latest pope's bastard . . . (*To Gabriel.*) Slip them three coins and tell them your name.

GABRIEL (*throws the* sbirro *his purse*): Prince Gabriel of Bramante.

ASTOLPHE: Bramante! My first cousin! By Bacchus and the devil! There are no bastards in our family . . .

SBIRRI CAPTAIN (*receives Gabriel's purse and looks at the Tavern Keeper with hesitation*): If you pay the host for the broken furniture and spilled wine . . . things can be arranged . . . When the assassins are brought to trial, you gentlemen will appear.

ASTOLPHE: The hell you say! It is enough that we must take the trouble to cut them up . . . I do not want to hear about them anymore. (*Low to Gabriel.*) Something for the host, and it will be over with.

GABRIEL (*takes out another purse*): Must we bribe the *sbirri* and the witnesses as if we were the criminals?

ASTOLPHE: Yes, that is the general custom here.

TAVERN KEEPER (*refuses Gabriel's money*): No, my lord, I am not worried about the damages to my establishment. I know that Your Highness will pay me for them generously, and I am in no haste. But justice must be served. I want this troublemaker Astolphe to be arrested and put in prison until he pays me back what he has owed me for six months. Besides, I am sick of the noise and brawls he and his bad company bring here every night. He has given my place a bad name . . . He is always the one who provokes quarrels. I am sure it was he who caused tonight's commotion . . .

A CUTTHROAT (*held down*): True, we were quietly keeping to ourselves . . .

ASTOLPHE (*in a thundering voice*): Will you not lie still in the dirt, you filthy vermin?[9] (*To Tavern Keeper.*) Ah! Ah! Given the gentleman's place a bad name! (*Bursts into laughter.*) Besmirching the reputation of the gentleman's den of cutthroats! This is a murderer's hideout . . . a bandit's cave . . .

TAVERN KEEPER: And you, sir, what brought you here to this bandit's cave?

ASTOLPHE: Business the police fail to do, which is to purge the earth of some cutthroats.

---

[9] Astolphe again employs *vous* to address the cutthroat, possibly to create an ironic contrast with the word "vermin" or, just as possibly, to establish distance from him.

SBIRRO: Lord Astolphe, the police do their job.

ASTOLPHE: Well stated, honorable sir, and the proof is that without our weapons and courage we would have been murdered just moments ago.

TAVERN KEEPER: That is what we need to find out. It is up to the courts to decide. Men of law and order, do your duty, or I will file a complaint.

SBIRRI CAPTAIN (*with a dignified air*): The police know what must be done. Come with us, Lord Astolphe.

TAVERN KEEPER: I have nothing to say against these noble gentlemen. (*Indicates Gabriel and Marc.*)

GABRIEL (*to* sbirri): Gentlemen, I shall follow you. If your duty is to arrest Lord Astolphe, then mine is to put myself in the hands of justice as well. If it is a crime to defend one's life against brigands, I am an accessory to his crime. One of the bodies that lay here earlier perished by my own hand.

ASTOLPHE: Brave cousin!

TAVERN KEEPER: You, his cousin? Well, now! Such insolence! A wretch who does not pay his debts!

GABRIEL: Quiet, sir, my cousin's debts will be paid. My bursar will come by here tomorrow morning.

TAVERN KEEPER (*bows*): That will be quite acceptable, my lord.

ASTOLPHE: You are wrong, cousin; my debt should be paid with the blows of a stick. I have got plenty others to which you ought to have given priority.

GABRIEL: All will be paid.

ASTOLPHE: I must be dreaming . . . Did I say my prayers this morning? Or did my good mother pay to have a mass said for me?

SBIRRI CAPTAIN: In that case, the matter can be taken care of . . .

GABRIEL: No, honorable sir, justice must not be compromised; take us to prison . . . Keep the money, and treat us well.

SBIRRI CAPTAIN: After you, my lord.

MARC (*to Gabriel*): What are you thinking of? You, my lord, in prison?

GABRIEL: Yes, I want to experience a little of everything.

MARC: Good God! What will his lordship your grandfather say?

(GABRIEL: He will say I am acting like a man.)

Scene 2

In prison.

Gabriel, Astolphe, *Sbirri* Captain, Marc.

Astolphe sleeps, stretched out on a prison cot. Marc dozes on a bench upstage. Gabriel paces slowly, slows down to look at Astolphe each time he passes him.

GABRIEL: He sleeps as though he had never lived anywhere else! Unlike me, he feels no horrible repugnance for these walls sullied with profanity, for this cot where murderers and parricides have rested their cursed heads. It is probably not the first night he has ever spent in prison! How strangely calm he is! And yet he took the life of his fellow man an hour ago! His fellow man! A ruffian? Yes, his fellow man. With wealth and good breeding, that ruffian might have been a brave officer, a great captain. Who could know, and who cares? Only someone for whom good breeding and capricious pride have created a destiny so contrary to nature's intention: myself! I, too, just killed a man . . . a man who by a similar chance could have been shrouded in a monk's robe from birth and cast forever into the calm and retiring life of the cloister! (*Looks at Astolphe.*) How strange that the circumstance of our first encounter made each of us commit murder! A dark omen! But I am the only one who worries about it, as if my soul were indeed of a different nature . . . No, I cannot accept a notion of inferiority that men alone have created but that God condemns. I shall be as stoic as those two, who sleep after a scene of murder and carnage. (*Throws himself on another bed.*)

ASTOLPHE (*dreaming*): Ah! deceitful Faustina! You are going to dine with Alberto, because he won my money from me! . . . I . . . despise you . . .[10] (*Awakens and sits up on his pallet.*) What a stupid dream! and a stupider awakening! Prison! Hey! Comrades? . . . No answer; everyone seems to be sleeping. Good night! (*Lies down again and goes to sleep.*)

GABRIEL (*rises, looks at him*): Faustina! That must be the name of his mistress. He dreams of his mistress, and I can think only of that man whose face contracted hideously when my bullet struck him . . . I did not see him die . . . I think he was still wheezing slightly when the police carried him out . . . I looked away . . . I could not have stood to look one more time at his bloody mouth, his smashed head! . . . I had never thought death could be so horrible. Was that ruffian's life less precious than my own? My own life! Is it not forever wretched? Is it not also criminal? My God! Forgive me. I saved the other one's life . . . I would not have had the courage to take his, as well . . . And that one! . . . who sleeps there so soundly, he would not have had mercy; he did not want to let any of them escape! Was that courage? Or brutality?

ASTOLPHE (*dreaming*): Help! Help me! I am being murdered . . . (*Moves fitfully on his pallet.*) Bastards! Six against

---

[10]Because Astolphe is using *tu* while addressing Faustina in his sleep, Gabriel can deduce that they are on familiar terms with each other.

one! . . . I am losing all my blood! . . . God, God! (*Awakens yelling.*)

Marc awakens with a start and runs about wildly. Astolphe gets up wildly and takes him by the throat. Both shout and wrestle with each other. Gabriel throws himself between them.

GABRIEL: Stop, Astolphe! Wake up: it is a dream! . . . You mistreat my elderly servant. (*Shakes him awake.*)

ASTOLPHE (*falls on his bed and wipes his brow*): What a hideous nightmare! Yes, I know perfectly who you are, now! I am drenched in a cold sweat. The wine I drank tonight was dreadful. Pay no attention to me. (*Lies down to go back to sleep.*)

Gabriel throws his coat on Astolphe and sits back on his bed.

✦ GABRIEL: Ah! So others dream, too! . . . So they, too, experience uneasiness, confusion, fear . . . at least in dreams! Their heavy sleep is only the result of a coarser disposition . . . or a sturdier constitution. It is not due to a stronger soul, or a calmer imagination. I do not know why the storm that passed over him has given me a serenity of sorts. I think I can sleep now . . . My God, you are my only friend! . . . Ever since the fateful day that terrible secret was revealed to me, not once have I fallen asleep without putting my soul in your hands, and asking you for justice and truth! . . . You owe more help and protection to me than to any other, because mine is a singular misfortune! . . . (*Falls asleep.*)

ASTOLPHE (*gets up again*): Impossible to sleep in peace; horrifying images assail my brain. Better for me to stay awake or drink a bottle of the wine the charitable guard slid under here, moved to tears by the youth and gold coins of my young cousin . . . (*Searches under the benches, ending up near Gabriel's pallet.*) This child sleeps like an angel! Well, well! It is good, at his age, to sleep after a little adventure like tonight's. By God, he killed his man more easily than I did! As if it were nothing . . . The blood of old Jules flows in those fine blue veins, beneath that skin so white! . . . A handsome boy, really! Raised like a maiden in a secluded old castle, by an elderly pedagogue spouting Latin and Greek. Or so I was told . . . Apparently, such an upbringing is as good as any other. Hold on, now! Must I melt like the tavern keeper and the guard because he promised to pay my debts? Certainly not! I will still speak frankly to him. Yet I feel that I like the boy. I like bravery in a delicate physique. It is not to my credit that I am fearless, with my peasant's muscles! This lad is probably satisfied drinking nothing but water! If I believed it, I would drink some, too, if only to enjoy that angelic sleep! But, since there is none here . . . (*Takes the bottle, then puts it down.*) Well, now! What has got into me that I keep looking at him? With his fifteen or sixteen years, and his chin smooth like a woman's, he almost makes you imagine . . . I would like to have a mistress who looks like him. But a woman can never have that kind of beauty, that mix of candor and strength, or at least the feeling of strength . . . His pink cheek is like a woman's, but his large, pure brow is a man's. (*Fills his glass and sits down, turning around every moment to look at Gabriel. Drinks.*) Faustina is a pretty girl . . . but despite her simpering ways, the creature's brazenness always shows through . . . Her laughter especially grates on my nerves. A courtesan's laugh! I dreamed she was dining with Alberto. Heaven knows she could do such a thing! (*Looks at Gabriel.*) If I had seen her sleep like that just once, I would be truly in love with her. But she is ugly when she sleeps! There seems to be something vile or cruel in her soul that she can get rid of when she talks or sings, but it comes back when sleep conquers her will . . . Ugh! This wine is the color of blood . . . and reminds me of my nightmare . . . Most certainly I am sick of wine, sick of women, sick of gambling . . . True, I am no longer thirsty, my pocket is empty, and I am in prison. But I am profoundly bored with the life I lead. And then, as my mother said, God will perform a miracle and I will become a saint. Oh! What do I see here? How very edifying! My little cousin wears a reliquary. If I could open very gently the collar of his shirt, cut the ribbon, and steal the amulet from him so that he must look for it when he wakes up . . .

Astolphe gently approaches Gabriel and extends his hand.
Gabriel awakens abruptly and draws his dagger.

GABRIEL: What do you want? Do not touch me, sir, or you are dead!

ASTOLPHE: What the devil! How savagely you wake, my handsome cousin! You almost stabbed my hand.

GABRIEL (*leaps from his pallet; curtly*): But what did you want from me? Whatever possessed you to wake me up with such a start? That was an extremely stupid joke.

ASTOLPHE: Oh, cousin! Do not let us be angry. I may be a stupid joker, but I do not much enjoy people telling me so. Really now, we should not have a falling out before we even know each other. If you want the truth, I was intrigued by the reliquary you wear around your neck . . . I was wrong, perhaps; but do not ask for an apology, I shall not give you any.

GABRIEL: If you want this bauble, I shall readily give it to you. My dying father put it around my neck, and for a long time I treasured it. But I have ceased of late to care much about it. Do you want it?

ASTOLPHE: No! What do you expect me to do with it? But are you aware that what you just said is not good? The memory of a father should be sacred to you.

GABRIEL: You may be right! but it may just be an abstraction! . . . To each his own!

ASTOLPHE: Well, even I would not harbor such thoughts, scoundrel though I am. I too was quite young when I lost my father. But I treasure everything I have that was his.

GABRIEL: I can believe that!

ASTOLPHE: You pay little attention to this conversation. Are you anxious about something? Put yourself at ease! Maybe you are tired! Drink a goblet of wine. It is not too bad for prison wine.

GABRIEL: I never drink wine.

ASTOLPHE: Just as I thought! If you do not, then your beard will never grow, my dear child.

GABRIEL: That may well be, but a beard does not a man make.

ASTOLPHE: It still helps considerably. However, you are entitled to speak as you do. Your chin is as smooth as the palm of my hand, and yet I do believe you are braver than I am.

GABRIEL: You think so?

ASTOLPHE: Funny boy! All the same, a little bit of beard would look good on you. You will see, women will look at you differently.

GABRIEL (*shrugs*): Women?

ASTOLPHE: Yes. Do you not like women, either?

GABRIEL: I cannot stand them.

ASTOLPHE (*laughs*): Ha, ha! What a character! So what do you like? Greek, rhetoric, geometry, what?

GABRIEL: None of all that. I like my horse, the open air, music, poetry, solitude, and above all freedom.

ASTOLPHE: How charming! But I would have thought you had the mind of a thinker.

GABRIEL: I do, somewhat.

ASTOLPHE: But I hope you are not self-centered?

GABRIEL: I do not know.

ASTOLPHE: What! Do you not love anyone? Do you not have a single friend?

GABRIEL: Not yet, but I wish I could have you for a friend.

ASTOLPHE: Me! You are very obliging, but how do you know if I am worthy of your friendship?

GABRIEL: I want you to be worthy of it. I should think you would have to be, considering what I plan to be for you.

ASTOLPHE: Oh! Slow down, slow down, cousin. You spoke of paying my debts, and I said, "Go ahead, if it pleases you," but now I tell you, "No posing as my protector, please, and especially no sermons." I am not particularly worried about paying my debts. And if you pay them, I certainly cannot promise I shall not accumulate more. My creditors will decide. I know very well that for the sake of family honor, it would be better if I were a proper gentleman, and did not frequent taverns and bad places, and indulged my vices discreetly . . .

GABRIEL: So you think it is for the sake of family honor that I offer you my assistance?

ASTOLPHE: It may be. People in our family do a lot of things out of pride.

GABRIEL: And even more out of bitterness.

ASTOLPHE: What do you mean?

GABRIEL: People in our family hate each other, and it is very sad indeed.

ASTOLPHE: I do not hate anyone, I daresay. Fate made you a sensible rich man and me a poor profligate. Perhaps it was too partial. It ought to have put more of the Jules' thrift and prudence into the blood of the Octaves, and a bit of the Octaves' carelessness and gaiety into the blood of the Jules. But in the end, if you are as melancholy and proud as you seem, I prefer my good humor and high spirits to your boredom and wealth. As you see, I have no reason to hate you, since I have no reason to envy you.

GABRIEL: Listen, Astolphe, you are wrong about me. I am indeed disposed to melancholy, but not pride. My parents' example would have been enough to cure me of any prideful tendencies I might have had. You called me a thinker. Well, so I am, enough to despise and renounce that particular delusion that substitutes isolation, hatred, and unhappiness for union, kindness, and happiness among kin.

ASTOLPHE: Well put. In that case, I accept your friendship. But will you not fall out of favor with my great-uncle, the old prince, if you keep company with me?

GABRIEL: Most certainly that will happen.

ASTOLPHE: If so, then let us go no further; take my word for it. I thank you for your good intentions, and you can count on having in me a cousin full of esteem for you, always ready and anxious for the opportunity to be of service in any circumstance. But do not trouble your life for a storybook friendship from which I would reap all the joys and benefits, while you reaped all the struggle and misfortune. That, I do not wish.

GABRIEL: But I do, Astolphe. Listen to me. A week ago I was still a child. Raised in an old manor house with a tutor, a library, falcons, and dogs, I knew nothing about our family quarrel and the hatred that divided our fathers. I did not hear anyone speak your name, nor did I even know of your existence. I received such an upbringing to be prevented from having my own ideas or feelings, I suppose. It was thought that I could be inculcated all at once with inherited hatred and pride, by learning, in one serious lecture, that I, though a child, was the head, the hope, the pillar of an illustrious family of which you were the enemy, the burden, and the shame.

ASTOLPHE: Old Jules said that? Oh, the base insolence of the wealthy!

GABRIEL: Leave the old man in peace. He is being punished enough by the sadness, fear, and boredom that consume his last days. When they told me all these things, when they told me that by right of birth I must constantly push you down, rejoice over your humiliation, and glory in your abjection, I ordered my horse to be saddled and my old servant to follow me. I took with me the money my grandfather had intended me to spend on traveling to various royal courts in order to learn how to become ambitious. I came looking for you so we could both spend this money on the pleasures of youth, or on learning together from our travels, however you like. I told myself that my frankness would convince you and remove any vain scruple you might have; that you would understand the need I have to love and be loved; that you would share with me like a brother; and finally that you would not force me to lead a life of pride, by showing yourself proud as well and rejecting a sincere heart that seeks you out and implores you.

ASTOLPHE (*embraces him warmly*): Upon my word, you are a noble child.[11] There is more resolution, wisdom, and rectitude in your young head than there ever was in

---

[11] In this speech, Astolphe uses *tu* with Gabriel for the first time, signaling the new sentiment of trust and affection that he feels. Gabriel continues to address Astolphe as *vous* for somewhat longer in the scene.

our whole family. Very well, I accept. We will be brothers and lay to rest the old quarrels of our fathers. As we travel the world together, we will each make concessions to remain ever in harmony: I will be a bit less wild, you a bit less restrained. Your grandfather cannot disinherit you: you will let yourself be scolded, but we will cherish each other right under his nose. The only revenge I will take for his hatred is to love you with all my soul.

GABRIEL (*shakes his hand*): Thank you, Astolphe; you have lifted a great burden from my shoulders.

ASTOLPHE: So it was to meet me that you came to the tavern tonight?

GABRIEL: I had been told that you were there every night.

ASTOLPHE: Dear Gabriel! And you almost got murdered in that squalid place! And without your help I too might have been killed! Ah! I shall never again expose you to such sordid dangers. I have the feeling I shall care for you as I have never cared for myself. United with yours, my life will seem more precious.

GABRIEL (*approaches the window bars*): Look! Daylight has come: look, Astolphe, how the waves redden as they bear forth the rising sun.[12] May our friendship be as pure, as beautiful as the day heralded by this brilliant dawn!

---

[12] Gabriel uses the second-person familiar form of the imperative verb *look*, signaling his switch from *vous* to *tu* when addressing Astolphe.

The jailor and Sbirri Captain enter.

SBIRRI CAPTAIN: My lords, upon learning your names, the chief of police has ordered that you be released immediately.

ASTOLPHE: So much the better. Freedom is always welcome, like good wine: you need not wait for thirst to enjoy it.

GABRIEL: Up, old Marc, wake up. Our captivity is over.

MARC (*low to Gabriel*): What! My dear master, are you going to leave arm in arm with Lord Astolphe? . . . What will His Highness say if someone tells him . . .

GABRIEL: His Highness is in for many other surprises. Just as I promised him, I shall act like a man!

ACT 2

Scene 1

In Astolphe's home.

Astolphe, wearing a fancy costume, is in the final stage of dressing and grooming before a large mirror. Faustina, elaborately dressed and bejeweled, enters on tiptoe and looks at him. Astolphe very carefully tries on various items of decorative head wear.

FAUSTINA (*aside*): Has a woman ever preened so much, and beheld her image with such pleasure? What a fop!

ASTOLPHE (*sees Faustina in the mirror; aside*): Good! I see you quite well, plague of my purse, enemy of my salvation! Ah! You have come back looking for me! Now it is my turn to bedevil you. (*Throws down an article of head wear with mock impatience and resumes meticulously arranging his hair.*)

FAUSTINA (*sits down and looks at him; aside again*): I must hold my own with him! Admire yourself, pretty lad! (And

they say women are the ones who care about their looks!)
He will not even deign to turn around.

ASTOLPHE: (*aside*): I wager she is getting impatient. Ha!
I shall do this for a bit longer. (*Tries on different headpieces
again.*)

FAUSTINA (*aside*): Again! . . . The fact is, he is handsome, much more handsome than Antonio. People can
say what they like, but nothing is more prestigious than
being on the arm of a handsome suitor. It dresses you up
more than all the jewels in the world. What a shame that
all these Alcibiades run out of money so quickly![13] This
one here no longer has means to give a woman even a
belt buckle or ribbon!

ASTOLPHE (*pretends to talk to himself*): One cannot put a
feather this way on a barrette! People who do that always
fancy they have hair like the students of Pavia![14] (*Pulls out
the feather and throws it on the floor.*)

Faustina picks it up.

FAUSTINA (*aside*): A magnificent feather! and the cos-
tumer will make him pay for it. But where does he get the

---

[13] Alcibiades (c. 450 BC–404 BC), a handsome, wealthy, and courageous Athenian general and politician who despite his abilities
was notorious for his passionate, insolent nature and a capacity for
deception that may have been the cause of his downfall.

[14] The students of Pavia had a reputation for licentiousness.

money to rent such expensive clothes? (*Looks around.*) But! I had not noticed before! How this apartment has changed! What luxury! This is a palace now. Mirrors! Paintings! (*Looks at the sofa where she is seated.*) A brand-new piece of velvet furniture with fine gold trim! Did he come into an inheritance? Good heavens, and for the past week I have been . . . I must be blind! Such a handsome boy! . . . (*Takes a small mirror from her pocket and arranges her hair.*)

ASTOLPHE (*aside*): Ah, she does all that for nothing. I am on the path of virtue.

FAUSTINA (*rises and goes to him*): Do as you like, you traitor! So when will the handsome Narcissus deign to turn his face away from the mirror?

ASTOLPHE (*without turning*): Oh, is that you, my dear girl?

FAUSTINA: Drop that patronizing tone and look at me.

ASTOLPHE (*without turning*): What do you want from me? I am pressed for time.

FAUSTINA (*pulls his arm*): Come now, do you not recognize my voice, Astolphe? You are riveted to your mirror!

ASTOLPHE (*turns slowly and looks at her with an indifferent air*): Well, what is it? I see you. You are not badly dressed. Where are you spending the night?

FAUSTINA (*aside*): Spite? Jealousy will take him down a peg. Let us show some confidence. (*Aloud.*) I am dining at Ludovic's.

ASTOLPHE: I am pleased to hear it. That is where I am going too in a little while.

FAUSTINA: That explains your expensive costume. It will be a magnificent party. The most beautiful girls of the city have been invited. Each gentleman is escorting his mistress. And you can see that my costume is not in bad taste.

ASTOLPHE: It is a bit shabby! Is that Antonio's taste? I do not recognize his customary generosity. My poor Faustina, could it be that he is starting to lose interest in you?

FAUSTINA: It is rather I who am starting to lose interest in him.

ASTOLPHE (*tries on gloves*): Poor boy!

FAUSTINA: You pity him?

ASTOLPHE: Quite. He has had a streak of bad luck. His uncle died last week. And at the hunt this morning a wild boar ripped apart the best of his dogs.

FAUSTINA: My luck is just as bad. This morning my chambermaid broke my Japanese porcelain figurine, my parrot died of food poisoning the day before yesterday, and I have not seen you all week.

ASTOLPHE (*pretends not to have heard correctly*): What did you say about Angélique?[15] I dined at her place yesterday. And where are you dining tomorrow?

FAUSTINA: With you.

---

[15] In the original text, the name is *Célimène*, which rhymes with *semaine*, the French word for "week."

ASTOLPHE: You think so?

FAUSTINA: It is a fancy I have.

ASTOLPHE: I have a different one.

FAUSTINA: Which is?

ASTOLPHE: To go to the country with a charming creature I won over recently.

FAUSTINA: Ah, ha! Eufémia, no doubt.

ASTOLPHE: Hardly!

FAUSTINA: Angélique?

ASTOLPHE: Ah, bah!

FAUSTINA: Francesca?

ASTOLPHE: Thank you very much!

FAUSTINA: Well, then, who? Someone I do not know.

ASTOLPHE: No one around here knows her yet. She is a young woman just arrived from her village. Beautiful as love, timid as a doe, good and faithful as . . .

FAUSTINA: As you?

ASTOLPHE: Yes, as me. And that is saying a lot, because I am hers for life.

FAUSTINA: I congratulate you . . . And we shall be seeing her tonight, I hope?

ASTOLPHE: I do not think so . . . But who knows? (*Aside.*) Oh, what a good idea! (*Aloud.*) Yes, I would like to take her to Ludovic's. As an artist, the brave man will be grateful to me for showing him this masterpiece of nature, and he will want to make her statue right away . . . But I shall not consent to it. I am jealous of my treasure.

FAUSTINA: Be careful this one does not slip away like your money did. In that case, good-bye. I came here to invite you to accompany me this evening. I wanted to play a dirty trick on Antonio. But since you have a lady, I will go find Menrique, who is mad about me.

ASTOLPHE (*with some emotion*): Menrique? (*Immediately recovers.*) You could not do better. Good-bye, then!

FAUSTINA: (*aside while exiting*): Bah! He has never been so broke. He must have pawned the last bit of his inheritance for his new passion. In a week, the lord will be in prison and the girl in the street. (*Exits.*)

Scene 2

ASTOLPHE (*alone*): With Menrique! To think I was stupid enough to admit to him I had almost taken that girl seriously . . . One word, and I could get her to come back . . . (*Goes to the door, then returns.*) No, that would be weakness. Gabriel would scorn me, rightfully so. My good Gabriel! Charming character! Amiable companion! How he always gives in to my whims, he who has none, and is so good, so pure! He watches me carry on this foolish life without getting annoyed or sanctimonious! He never criticizes me. And whenever I express the slightest wish, he responds immediately and gets me money, horses and carriages, a mistress, luxuries of all kinds. At the very least, I wish he could share in the fun. But I suspect he does not enjoy all this, and that his occasional show of cheerfulness is just a heroic act of friendship. Oh! If I were sure of it, I would reform right now. I would buy books, immerse myself in the classics, go to confession, what would I not do for him! . . . What a long time he takes to get dressed. (*Goes to knock on the door leading to Gabriel's rooms.*) Well, my friend, are you ready? Not yet. Let me come in, I am alone. No? Oh, come now! Very well, as you wish. (*Comes back.*) He locks himself in there just like a young girl. He wants me to get the full effect of his costume. I am sure he will be charming dressed as a girl. Faustina did not see him. She will be fooled, and all the women will be consumed with jealousy. It was hard, though, for him to agree to this nonsense. Dear Gabriel! I am the one who is a child, and he is the man, a wise man full of indulgence and devotion! (*Rubs his hands.*) Ah! I shall enjoy myself at Faustina's expense! What an impudent creature! Last week Antonio, today Menrique! How quickly women descend into a career of vice! We men know we can always stop ourselves. But nothing can keep women from sliding down the fatal slope. And when we try to help them up, we only hasten their fall into the abyss. My friends are right. I am the least rakish of all, I who pass for the worst fellow in town. I have sentimental tendencies, I dream of romantic love. And when I clasp a vile creature in my arms, I wish I could imagine myself in love with her. Antonio must have made such fun of me with that despicable fool! I should have kept her tonight, and gone out with both her and Gabriel in his costume, singing the refrain, "Better two women than one." I would have spited Antonio with Faustina and Faustina with Gabriel . . . Wait! Perhaps there is still time . . . She lied, she would not have dared go get Menrique like that . . . She is not so bold! While Gabriel completes his disguise, I can run to her place, it is not far. (*Wraps himself in his coat.*) How can a woman descend so low that she becomes no more than an object for our vanity to show off like clothes or a piece of furniture! (*Exits.*)

Scene 3

Gabriel, dressed as a very elegant woman, slowly emerges from his room. Périnne follows him with an air of avid curiosity.

GABRIEL: Fine, thank you, Périnne; I no longer need you.[16] This is for your trouble. (*Gives her money.*)

PÉRINNE: My lord, you are too kind. Your Lordship will please all the women young and old, rich and poor, for in addition to what heaven blessed you with, you are of such noble generosity that . . .

GABRIEL: Fine, fine, Périnne. Good evening.

---

[16] Gabriel uses *vous*, because Périnne is a serving woman whom he just met, unlike the servant Marc, whom he has known since birth.

PÉRINNE (*puts the money in her pocket*): This is really too much! Your Highness did not allow me to help him . . . I only attached the belt and the bracelets. If I dared give a last word of advice to Your Excellency, I would say that your lace collar is worn too high. You have the round white neck of a woman; the shoulders would have a good effect under this transparent veil. (*Tries to arrange the lace.*)

Gabriel pushes her away.

GABRIEL: Enough, I tell you. A little diversion must not become such a serious task. I am quite satisfied.

PÉRINNE: Yes indeed! I know more than one great lady who would like to have Your Highness's fine waistline and alabaster skin! (*Gabriel impatiently waves her away; Périnne bows grandly and ridiculously; aside.*) I do not understand it. He is made to perfection, but what fanatical prudery! He must be a Huguenot![17]

Scene 4

GABRIEL (*alone, approaches the mirror*): How I suffer in this garment! Everything binds and stifles me. The corset is torture, and I feel so awkward! . . . I still dare not look at

---

[17] For an anglophone theatrical audience, one might consider the word "Puritan" as a substitute.

myself. I was frozen with fear by that old woman's curious eye! . . . Though I would have been unable to dress without her. (*Goes before the mirror and gives a cry of surprise.*) My God! Is that me? She said I would make a beautiful girl . . . Is it true? (*Looks at himself in silence for a long time.*) Women like that give praises for money . . . What if Astolphe finds me clumsy and ridiculous? The costume is indecent . . . The sleeves are too short! . . . Ah! I have gloves! . . . (*Puts on his gloves and pulls them above his elbows.*) What a strange idea of his. It seems so simple to him! . . . And I was mad enough to indulge a reckless desire to undertake this experiment, despite my repugnance for putting on such clothing! . . . How will I appear to him? I must be ungraceful! . . . (*Tries a few steps in front of the mirror.*) Yet it does not seem so difficult. (*Tries working the fan and breaks it.*) Oh! I do not understand a thing about this. Can a woman not be pleasing without these simpering affectations? (*Remains absorbed before the mirror.*)

Scene 5

Astolphe reenters quietly while Gabriel stands before the mirror.

ASTOLPHE (*aside*): That miserable woman lied to me! She will be going with Antonio! I do not want Gabriel to know that I did such a stupid thing. (*Closing the door quietly,*

he turns around and notices Gabriel, whose back is turned.)
What do I see! Who is this beautiful girl? . . . What!
Gabriel! . . . I did not recognize you, I swear it! (*Gabriel,
very flustered, blushes and loses composure.*) Ah! My God!
But it is a dream! How beautiful you are! . . . Gabriel, is
that you? . . . Do you have a twin sister? It cannot be . . .
my child! . . . my dear! . . .

GABRIEL (*very frightened*): What is the matter, Astolphe?
You look at me strangely.

ASTOLPHE: But how do you expect me not to be moved?
Look at yourself. Do you not take yourself for a girl?

GABRIEL (*flustered*): Then, Périnne disguised me well?

ASTOLPHE: Périnne is a fairy godmother. With a wave
of her magic wand she has changed you into a woman. It
is remarkable. If I had seen you like that the first time we
met, I would never have guessed your sex . . . Indeed! I
would have fallen head over heels in love.

GABRIEL (*with feeling*): Truly, Astolphe?

ASTOLPHE: As true as I am forever your brother and
your friend, you would have immediately become my
mistress and my wife if . . . How you blush, Gabriel! But
do you know you blush like a young girl? . . . You did
not put on makeup, I hope? (*Touches her cheeks.*) No! You
tremble?

GABRIEL: I am not used to such light fabrics and feel
chilly.

ASTOLPHE: Cold! Your hands burn! . . . You are not ill? . . . What a child you are, my little Gabriel! You are flustered by this disguise. If I did not know you to be a thinker, I would suppose you were extremely devout and contemplating an enormous sin . . . Oh! What fun we shall have! All the men will be in love with you, and the women will want to scratch your eyes out with spite. Such beautiful dark eyes Your Ladyship has! I do not know what has come over me. You have put me under such a spell that I no longer dare speak to you without deference![18] . . . Ah! Gabriel! Why is there no woman who resembles you?

GABRIEL: You are mad, Astolphe; you think of nothing but women.

ASTOLPHE: And what the devil do you expect me to think about at my age? I simply cannot conceive how you do not think about them yet!

GABRIEL: Yet you told me just this morning you hated them.

ASTOLPHE: No doubt I hate all those I know; because I only know disreputable ones.

GABRIEL: Why do you not look for a sweet, honest girl? A person whom you could marry and love forever.

---

[18] A more literal translation would be, "I dare not use *tu* with you anymore." Astolphe has just half-ironically and half-seriously used the *vous* form while admiring Gabriel's eyes, a formality we conveyed by having him call Gabriel "Your Ladyship."

ASTOLPHE: Honest girls! Ah! Yes, I know some. But just seeing them pass by on their way to church makes me yawn. What do you want me to do with a little fool who only knows how to embroider and make the sign of the cross? Some are flirts and mischievous sorts who cast a smoldering glance at you the whole time they reach for holy water. Those kinds are worse than our courtesans, for they are vain and unchaste, which is to say, venal and hypocritical. Better a Faustina who brazenly tells you, "I'm going to Menrique's or Antonio's," than the woman reputed to be honest who swears eternal love and then cheats on you from one day to the next.

GABRIEL: If you despise members of the other sex so much, then no wonder you cannot love them!

ASTOLPHE: But I love women out of need. I yearn for love! In my dreams, in my heart is an ideal woman! And that woman resembles you, Gabriel. An intelligent and simple being, upright and refined, brave and shy, generous and proud. I see this woman's face in my dreams. I see her tall, pale, blond, like you right now with your beautiful dark eyes and that silky, perfumed hair. Do not make fun of me, my friend. Let me get carried away; it is carnival time. Everyone tries to create the image of what he desires to be or to possess: the valet dresses as a master, the imbecile as a doctor. In my case, I have dressed you up as a woman. Poor as I am, I have created an imaginary treasure for myself, and I gaze at you with a mixture of sadness and elation. I know well that tomorrow your pretty feet will disappear in boots, and that your hand will shake mine roughly and fraternally. In the meantime, if I had my way, I would kiss this hand so soft . . . Really, your hand is no bigger than a woman's, and your arm . . . Let me kiss your glove! . . . Your arm is miraculously round . . . See here, my dear beautiful lady, you are so exquisitely virtuous! . . . My, my! You play your role like an angel: you roll up your gloves, you tremble, you lose your composure. Marvelous! Let us see, walk a bit, take little steps.

GABRIEL (*tries to laugh*): You must make me walk and speak as little as possible; for I have a husky voice, and I must not be very graceful, either.

ASTOLPHE: Your voice is full, but soft. Few women have one so pleasant. And as for your walk, I assure you it is adorably awkward. I will pass you off as an innocent young maid. So do not worry about your manners.

GABRIEL: But certainly your ideal woman has better ones?

ASTOLPHE: Ha! Not at all. I see you and realize that your awkwardness is a more powerful attraction than all the skills of elegant women. Your costume is charming! Was it Périnne who chose it?

GABRIEL: No! She brought me a Gypsy outfit the other day. I had her make this white silk dress especially for me.

ASTOLPHE: And you will be more adorned, with this simple attire and pearls, than all the motley plumed women getting ready to compete with you for the prize. But who put that crown of white roses on your forehead? Do you know you resemble the marble angels of our cathedrals? Who gave you the idea for this costume so simple, yet so refined?

GABRIEL: A dream that I had . . . some time ago.

ASTOLPHE: Aha! So you dream of angels? Well, do not wake up, because in real life you will find only women! My poor Gabriel, never fall in love, if you can help it. What woman would be worthy of you? I get the feeling that the day you are in love, I shall be sad and jealous.

GABRIEL: But should I not be jealous of the women you chase after?

ASTOLPHE: Oh! You would be making a big mistake! There would be no reason! Someone knocks downstairs! . . . Quickly, get into character. (*Listens to the voices of people coming up the stairs.*) Good God! It is Antonio with Faustina. They are coming to get us. Quickly put on your mask! . . . your coat! . . . a pink satin coat lined with swan's down! Charming! . . . Let us go, dear Gabriel! Now that I no longer see your face and arms, I can remember that you are my comrade . . . Come! . . . Liven up a bit. Let us go and enjoy ourselves!

They exit.

74

Scene 6

At Ludovic's. A half-lit boudoir adjoining a very
rich gallery; through the upstage entrance,
a sparkling salon.

*Gabriel, disguised as a woman, sits on the sofa. Astolphe
enters with Faustina on his arm.*

FAUSTINA (*in a biting tone*): A boudoir? Oh, how pretty!
But there are too many of us here.

GABRIEL (*coldly*): Madam is right, and I yield her my
place. (*Rises.*)

FAUSTINA: I can tell you are not the jealous type!

ASTOLPHE: She would have no cause for jealousy! I have
already told her she can feel secure.

GABRIEL: I am neither especially jealous nor secure; but
I yield before madam.

FAUSTINA: Please do stay, madam.

ASTOLPHE: Please call her miss, not madam.

FAUSTINA (*bursts out laughing*): Ah, well! Yes, miss! You
are a big fool, my poor Astolphe.

ASTOLPHE: Laugh as much as you like. If I could call
you miss, then perhaps I would still love you.

FAUSTINA: And I would be very put out. Such love would
be too insufferably boring. (*To Gabriel.*) Does platonic love
amuse you? (*Aside.*) Really, she blushes as if she were completely innocent. Where the devil did Astolphe find her?

ASTOLPHE: Faustina, do you believe in my word of honor?

FAUSTINA: Why, yes.

ASTOLPHE: Well then, I swear to you on my honor (and not on yours) that she is not my mistress, and that I respect her like my sister.

FAUSTINA: So you plan to make her your wife? In that case, you are a big fool to bring her here, for she will learn a lot of things she is not supposed to know.

ASTOLPHE: On the contrary, she will be horrified by the vice she sees in you and your kind.

FAUSTINA: No doubt it was to make her feel such profound horror that you brought me here with quite immoral intentions? Madam . . . or miss . . . Take my word for it, he was not expecting to find you on the sofa. I may have no word of honor, but your gentleman fiancé has one; make him swear! . . . so that he dares say why he brought me here! Then, you can stay; it is a lesson in virtue that Astolphe wants to give you.

GABRIEL (*to Astolphe*): I cannot tolerate such impudent speech another second; I am leaving.

ASTOLPHE (*whispers*): (How well you play along! You sound just like a very prudish young lady.) ⤵

GABRIEL (*low to Astolphe*): I assure you, I am not play-acting. All this revolts me; let me leave. You stay; do not interrupt your pleasures on my account.

ASTOLPHE: No, by the devil! I want to punish that goose's impertinence! (*Aloud.*) Fausta, go away, leave us. I wanted to get even with Antonio, but now that I have seen my fiancée, I can think of nothing but her. Many thanks for your willingness; good evening.

FAUSTINA (*furious*): You would deserve it if I trampled on the flowered crown of this so-called fiancée who has probably already had more husbands than the number of women you have betrayed. (*Approaches Gabriel menacingly.*)

ASTOLPHE (*pushes her*): Fausta! If you have the misfortune of touching a hair on her head, I will tie your hands behind your back, call my valet, and have your head shaved.[19]

Faustina falls onto the sofa, sobs convulsively. Gabriel approaches her.

GABRIEL: Astolphe, it is wrong to treat a woman like that. Look how she suffers!

ASTOLPHE: It is from anger, not pain. Do not worry, she is used to this affliction.

GABRIEL: Astolphe, that kind of anger is the worst of all suffering. You are the one who provoked her, so you do

---

[19] In many cultures, shaving heads was considered a particularly humiliating punishment for women. In Corinthians 1, it is suggested that women who do not wear the veil ought to have their hair cut off.

not have the right to rebuke her so harshly. Give her a comforting word. You brought her here to have fun, not to outrage her. (*Faustina pretends to faint.*) Madame, do collect yourself; it was all a joke. I am not a woman, I am Astolphe's cousin.[20]

ASTOLPHE: Gabriel, you really are mad!

FAUSTINA (*slowly recovers her spirits*): Really! You are the Prince of Bramante? How could this be! . . . Ah, but yes it is, I do recognize you. I saw you go by on horseback the other day. You ride better than Astolphe, better than Antonio himself, whose riding it was that first attracted me.

ASTOLPHE: Well, now! That was a proposition. I hope you understand, Gabriel, and that you will know how to press your advantage. Now there! Faustina, you are a good girl, do not betray the secret of our masquerade. You were fooled. Try not to be the only one, that would be embarrassing for you.

FAUSTINA: Heaven forbid! I want Antonio to be fooled, and as cruelly as possible, because he is already hopelessly in love with this gentleman. (*To Gabriel.*) Good! I see him now giving you sidelong glances from the back of the room. To keep up the hoax, I shall give you a hug.

---

[20]Unlike Astolphe, who uses *tu*, Gabriel uses *vous* to address Faustina.

GABRIEL (*recoils from the embrace*): No, no thank you! I would not want to follow in my cousin's footsteps.

FAUSTINA: Oh, how sure he is! Is he devout? Well, well, this pleases me to no end. My goodness, but he is pretty! Astolphe, you must still be in love with me, since you had not introduced him to me. You knew very well that just looking at him could be dangerous. Is that beautiful hair yours? And what hands! What a love!

ASTOLPHE (*to Faustina*): Good! Try to corrupt him. He is too chaste, you know! (*To Gabriel.*) Well! Let us see! She is beautiful, and you are handsome enough not to fear being loved for your money. I will leave you two alone together.

GABRIEL (*clings to Astolphe*): No, Astolphe, it would be no use. I could not bring myself to insult a woman, or to hold her in such low regard by accepting her that way.

FAUSTINA: Do not torment him, Astolphe, I know how to warm him up when I feel like it. Right now let us work on fooling Antonio. Here he comes, burning with love and trembling with hope, loitering and moping by this door. How bumbling and miserable he looks! Let us move a little closer to him.

GABRIEL (*to Astolphe*): Let me leave. I am tired of this joke. My dress is uncomfortable, and I do not like your Antonio!

FAUSTINA: All the more reason to make fun of him, my handsome cherub. Oh, Astolphe, if only you could have seen how Antonio followed your cousin while you danced the tarantella! He wanted so much to embrace him, and this angel defended himself with such well-feigned modesty!

ASTOLPHE: Come on, you can allow yourself to be hugged a bit for a joke. Where is the harm? Oh, Gabriel, please, do not leave us yet. If you do, then I too must leave, and it would be a shame, I do so want to enjoy myself!

GABRIEL: Then I shall stay.

FAUSTINA: What a pleasant child!

They exit. Antonio stops them in the gallery. After some conversation, Astolphe passes Gabriel's arm to Antonio's and follows them with Faustina, enjoying their joke. They go offstage.

Scene 7

Still at Ludovic's. A garden, light coming
from upstage.

Astolphe is very agitated; Gabriel runs after him.

GABRIEL (*still in a woman's costume, with a large white lace mantilla*): Astolphe, where are you going? What is the matter? You seem to be running away from me. Why?

ASTOLPHE: Nothing is the matter, my child. I want a breath of fresh air, nothing else. All the noise, all the wine and warm perfumes have gone to my head and begin to make me ill. If you want to leave, I will not stop you anymore. I will join you soon.

GABRIEL: Why not go home with me right now?

ASTOLPHE: I need to be alone here for a moment.

GABRIEL: I understand. Some woman again?

ASTOLPHE: Well, no; it concerns a duel, if you must know. If you were not in disguise, you could serve as my second, but I asked Menrique.

GABRIEL: And you think I would leave you? But with whom is the duel?

ASTOLPHE: You know very well: with Antonio.

GABRIEL: So it is not serious, and I should stay behind to let him know I am your cousin, not a woman.

ASTOLPHE: He would only be more furious that he was fooled in front of everyone. I am not waiting for him to challenge me, because he is the one who must make amends to me.

GABRIEL: My God, what for?

ASTOLPHE: He insulted you, and he insulted me. He forced you into a kiss right in front of me after I pretended to be jealous and told him to leave you alone.

GABRIEL: But since you invented this joke, you have no right to take it seriously.

ASTOLPHE: I do; I take it very seriously.

GABRIEL: If he was disrespectful, it was with me, and it is up to me to make him pay.

ASTOLPHE (*very moved, takes him by the arm*): You! As long as I live, you will never fight! My God! If I ever saw a man draw a sword against you, I would become a murderer, I would even strike him from behind. Ah! Gabriel, you have no idea how I love you. I do not even know myself.

GABRIEL (*uneasy*): You are quite carried away today, my dear brother.

ASTOLPHE: If you say so. Yet I was very sober at supper. Did you notice? Well, right now I feel more intoxicated than if I had been drinking three nights in a row.

GABRIEL: How strange! When you challenged Antonio, you were beside yourself. And I admired how well you played the part.

ASTOLPHE: I was not playing, I was furious! I still am. Just the thought of it makes the sweat break out on my brow.

GABRIEL: He did not say anything insulting to you, though. He laughed; everyone laughed.

ASTOLPHE: Except for you. You looked as though you were in agony.

GABRIEL: I played my role; that is all.

ASTOLPHE: You played it so well that I daresay I took mine seriously. Listen, Gabriel, I am not myself tonight. I am under the spell of a strange illusion: I am convinced that you are a woman. Even though I know otherwise, the illusion has taken hold of my imagination the way the reality does, perhaps even more so. Because when you are in that costume, I feel a passion for you that is jealous, ardent, fearful, and chaste. Surely I shall never feel this way again. The fancy has intoxicated me all evening. During supper, all eyes were upon you; all the men shared this illusion, they all wanted to touch the glass your lips had touched, and fetch the rose petals that fell from the garland in your hair. Everyone was spellbound! And I was drunk with pride, as if you really had been my fiancée! They say that Benvenuto brought his student, Ascanio, disguised as you are, to a supper at Michelangelo's, among the prettiest girls of Florence, and that the whole evening Ascanio was considered the most beautiful. I am sure he was less beautiful than you are, Gabriel . . . I looked at you in the candlelight with your white dress and your beautifully languorous arms that seemed to embarrass you, and your melancholy smile with its candor so different from the poorly concealed shamelessness on all the hussies' faces! . . . I was fascinated! Oh what power beauty and innocence have! That orgy became peaceful and almost chaste. The women wanted to imitate your reserve. The men were subdued by hidden feelings of respect. They stopped singing Aretino's verses,[21] no obscene word dared reach your ear . . . I had completely forgotten that you are not a woman . . . I was taken in, every bit as much as the others. And then that smug Antonio came along, with his bloodshot eyes and his lips still sullied by Faustina's kisses, and asked for a kiss, which even I would not have dared ask for . . . At that moment a thousand furies burned in my heart. I certainly would have killed him if people had not held me back, and I challenged him . . . And even now that the wine has worn off, I am astonished to feel that my madness would return if I saw him come near you.

GABRIEL: All this comes from tonight's exuberance at supper. It is for a good reason that people condemn this sort of entertainment. You see that it can stir up impure impulses, the very thought of which would have made our blood run cold. This game has lasted too long, Astolphe. I am leaving and will remove this dangerous disguise, never to wear it again.

ASTOLPHE: You are right, my Gabriel. Go, I will join you soon.

GABRIEL: But I will not leave unless you promise to renounce this mad quarrel and make peace with Antonio.

---

[21] Pietro Aretino (1492–1556) was known for pasquinades, lampoons, and licentious verses.

I asked Faustina to tell him the truth. You see, he is not coming for the duel and considers his honor satisfied.

ASTOLPHE: Well now, that angers me: I wished to fight with him! He stole Faustina from me. Not that I mind, but he did it to humiliate me. Any pretext would serve me well to punish him.

GABRIEL: That one would be ridiculous. And who knows? Mean-spirited people might read odious meanings into your behavior.

ASTOLPHE: That is true! So, away with my resentment, and away with my honor and bravado, for the sake of your spotless reputation . . . I promise to turn the whole thing into a joke.

GABRIEL: You give me your word?

ASTOLPHE: I swear it.

They shake hands.

GABRIEL: Here they come, laughing heartily. I shall slip away. (*Aside.*) It was high time, dear Lord! I am more distraught, more unsettled than he. (*Wraps himself in his mantilla, Astolphe helping him.*)

ASTOLPHE (*clasps him in his arms*): Ah! What a shame that you are a boy! All right, go. You will find your carriage at the bottom of the stairs, this way! . . .

Gabriel disappears beneath the trees while Astolphe's gaze follows him. Astolphe remains absorbed for a while. At the

sound of laughter from Antonio and Faustina, he passes
his hand over his forehead as if coming out of a dream.

Scene 8

Astolphe, Antonio, Faustina, Menrique, groups of
young men and courtesans.

ANTONIO: Ah! What a good story! I was outrageously deceived, but I feel better knowing I was not the only one.

MENRIQUE: Ah! You are right, I pined all through supper. Tonight when he takes off his dress, he'll find a love letter from me in his pocket.

FAUSTINA: That beautiful minx will have a good laugh at all of you men.

ANTONIO: And all of you women!

FAUSTINA: Except me. I recognized him right away.

ASTOLPHE (*to Antonio*): You are not too angry with me?

ANTONIO (*shakes his hand*): Oh, come now! I owe you a thousand praises. You played your role like a professional actor. Othello was never better performed.

MENRIQUE: But where did the handsome boy go? Now we can kiss him heartily on both cheeks.

ASTOLPHE: He went to get undressed, and I do not think he will return. But tomorrow I invite you all to lunch at my place with him.

FAUSTINA: Are the rest of us invited?

ASTOLPHE: No, to the devil with women!

Scene 9

Gabriel's room in Astolphe's apartments.

Gabriel, dressed as a woman and wrapped in his coat and veil, enters and awakens Marc, who sleeps on a chair.

MARC: Ah! I beg your pardon! . . . Madam wants Lord Astolphe. He has not returned . . . This is the room of Lord Gabriel.

GABRIEL (*throws his veil and coat on a chair*): So you do not recognize me, old Marc?

MARC (*rubs his eyes*): Good God! What is it I see? . . . As a woman, my lord, as a woman!

GABRIEL: Do not worry, old fellow, it is not for long. (*Tears off the head garland and eagerly messes up his hair.*)

MARC: As a woman! I am speechless! What would His Highness say? . . .

GABRIEL: Ah! this time His Highness would find that I did not act like a man. Go on now, Marc, go to bed. Tomorrow you will find me more like a boy than ever, I assure you! Good night, dear fellow.

Marc exits.

GABRIEL (*alone*): Quick, off with this Deianeira robe.[22]
It burns my chest, it thrills and confines me! Oh! what
turmoil, what a terrible mistake, my God! . . . But how
do I undo all this? . . . All these ties, all these pins . . .
(*Tears at his lace neckerchief and rips it off by pieces.*)
Astolphe, Astolphe, your turmoil will be over once I am
no longer in this disguise and have taken up the other
one, and the spell will be broken for you. But I, shall I
find under my doublet the same calm blood and innocent thoughts? . . . His last embrace consumed me! Ah!
I cannot undo this bodice! I must hurry! . . . (*Takes his
dagger from the table and cuts the laces.*) Now, where did
old Marc hide my doublet? My God! I think I hear someone coming up the stairs! (*Runs to bolt the door.*) He took
away my coat and veil! . . . The old sleepyhead! He did
not know what he was doing . . . And I wager the keys
to my trunks are still in his pocket . . . Nothing, not one
bit of clothing, and Astolphe will want to talk with me
when he returns . . . If I do not let him in, I will arouse
his suspicions! Damned foolishness! Ah! . . . before he

---

[22] According to Greek myth, Deianeira, the second wife of Hercules,
was captured by the centaur Nessus, and Hercules killed Nessus
with arrows dipped in poisonous blood. Before dying, Nessus told
Deianeira that blood from his wound would ensure Hercules's
fidelity to her. Later, she contrived to have Hercules don a robe
doused with the blood. The robe adhered to his skin, burning him
and causing him to die in agony.

comes in here, I must find a coat in his room . . . (*Takes a candlestick, opens a little side door, and enters the adjoining room.*)

An instant of silence, then a cry.

ASTOLPHE (*from the neighboring room*): Gabriel, you are a woman! Oh, dear God!

The candlestick drops, the light disappears. Gabriel returns distraught. Astolphe follows him in the darkness, stops at the threshold of the door.

ASTOLPHE: Have no fear, have no fear! From now on I do not pass through this door without your permission. (*Falls to his knees.*) My God, thank you!

ACT 3

In a small run-down old castle, belonging to
Astolphe and secluded deep in the woods, a dark
room with faded antique furniture.

Scene 1

Settimia and Barbe sew near one window, Gabrielle em-
broiders near the other; Brother Como goes from one to
the other, moving laboriously, and always stopping near
Gabrielle.

BROTHER COMO (*to Gabrielle in a low voice*): So, madam,
will you go hunting again tomorrow?[23]

GABRIELLE (*also in a low voice, cold and brusque*): Why
not, Brother Como, if my husband approves?

BROTHER COMO: Oh! You always answer in a way that
cuts short any conversation!

GABRIELLE: It is just that I do not care for idle chatter.

---

[23] The characters in this scene use *vous* to address one another.

BROTHER COMO: Well then, you will not put me off so easily, and I shall draw my own conclusions from your answer. (*Gabrielle remains silent: Brother Como continues.*) What I mean is that if I were Astolphe, I would not want to see you on horseback galloping furiously through the marshes and brush. (*Gabrielle remains silent; Brother Como lowers his voice progressively.*) Yes indeed! If I had the good fortune to possess a beautiful young wife, I would not want her to expose herself to such . . .

Gabrielle rises.

SETTIMIA (*in a curt and bitter voice*): You tire already of our company?

GABRIELLE: I saw Astolphe in the lane of chestnut trees. He waved to me, so I shall go join him.

BROTHER COMO (*in a low voice*): Shall I accompany you there?

GABRIELLE (*aloud*): I wish to go alone. (*Exits.*)

BROTHER COMO (*goes back to the others, sneering*): Did you hear her? You see how she treats me? Your Ladyship will have to dispense with my services in the task of her salvation. Her rebuffs are discouraging. She has a stubborn little mind, and she is full of pride. I have told you so a hundred times.

SETTIMIA: Your duty, Father, is never to get discouraged when your task is to bring a wandering soul back into the fold. I need not tell you that.

BARBE (*rises, puts her spectacles on her nose, and goes to examine Gabrielle's embroidery*): I knew it! Not a stitch since yesterday! You think that she works? All she does is break threads, lose needles, and waste silk. Look how tangled up all the threads are!

BROTHER COMO (*looks at her handiwork*): She is not without talent, though! Here is a very pretty flower that would go well in an altar frontal. Look at this flower, my sister Barbe! You yourself might not do any better.

BARBE (*bitterly*): I should be quite vexed with shame to do that. What use are all those beautiful flowers?

BROTHER COMO: She says it is to make a lining for her husband's coat.

SETTIMIA: What foolishness! As if her husband needed a silk embroidered lining when he does not even have enough money for a coat! She would do better to mend the household linens along with the rest of us.

BARBE: We cannot manage everything. What does she do to help us? Nothing!

SETTIMIA: And what is she good at? Nothing of any use. Ah! What bad fortune for me to have such a daughter-in-law! But my son has always given me nothing but grief.

BROTHER COMO: At least she seems to love her husband! . . . (*A silence.*) Do you think she loves her husband very much? (*Silence.*) Do you, my sister Barbe?

BARBE: Do not ask me about that. I do not concern myself with their affairs.

SETTIMIA: If she loved her husband, as would become a pious and well-behaved wife, she would concern herself a little more with his well-being instead of encouraging all his capricious whims and helping him spend money.

BROTHER COMO: Do they spend a lot?

SETTIMIA: Everything they can. What use do they have for two thoroughbred horses that eat day and night in the stable and lack the strength to pull a wagon or plow?

BARBE (*ironically*): They go hunting! Such a wonderful pastime, hunting!

SETTIMIA: Yes, a pastime for princes! But when you are ruined, you must cease to permit yourself such carryings-on.

BROTHER COMO: She rides a horse as well as Saint George.[24]

BARBE: Fie, Brother Como! Do not compare with the heavenly saints a person who does not go to confession and who reads all sorts of books.

SETTIMIA (*lets her work fall*): What! All sorts of books! Has she brought bad books into my house?

BARBE: Books in Greek, books in Latin. When such books are neither prayer books, nor the Gospels, nor by

---

[24] Saint George was known for chivalrous behavior as a knight on horseback. In the fifteenth century his feast day rivaled Christmas in popularity.

the Church Fathers, they can only be books by pagans or heretics! Look, here is one of the smaller ones that I put in my pocket to show you.

BROTHER COMO (*opens the book*): Thucydides! Oh! We permit this one in the schools . . . With some passages expunged, it is safe to read the pagan authors.[25]

SETTIMIA: That is all well and good, but when one reads only those, one is quite close to not believing in God. And did she not dare to maintain at supper yesterday that Dante was not a blasphemous author?

BARBE: She dared go further than that; she said that she did not believe in the damnation of heretics.

BROTHER COMO (*in a sanctimonious and dogmatic tone*): She said that? Ah! That is quite alarming! Quite serious indeed!

BARBE: Besides, does a modest woman jump fences with her horse?

SETTIMIA: When I was young, one mounted a horse, but with modesty. One did not put one's leg over the saddle. One followed the hunt with a bird on the wrist; but it was at a measured and cautious pace, and with a servant who ran along on foot while holding the horse by the

---

[25] Thucydides, a Greek historian and author of *History of the Pelopenesian War*, was sometimes called the father of modern history for attempting to evaluate empirical evidence instead of relying on myth or romance.

bridle. It was noble and decent. We did not come back disheveled. We never caught our lace on every branch in order to race with the men.

BROTHER COMO: Ah! In those days Your Ladyship had escorts in abundance and magnificent caparisons!

SETTIMIA: And I did honor to my fortune without committing the slightest extravagance. But heaven gave me an undisciplined, inconsiderate son who scorns good advice, follows every bad example, and throws away money right and left. And to cap off my bad fortune, just when I believed he had mended his ways, just when he was showing me more respect and tenderness, he goes and brings me a daughter-in-law whom I do not know, whom no one knows, who comes from God knows where, who has no fortune and perhaps even less family.

BROTHER COMO: She claims to be an orphan and the daughter of an honest gentleman?

BARBE: Who knows? You never hear her speak of her parents or her father's house.

BROTHER COMO: She seems to have been raised in wealth, to judge from her manners. She is some daughter of a great house who married your son in secret against her parents' wishes. Perhaps one day she will be rich.

SETTIMIA: That is what he wished to make me believe when he announced his plans to me. I did not stand in his way, because dissembling is not one of his vices. But

I see quite well now that this adventuress has taken him down the path of deception, because nothing backs up his claims. I have lived away from society for many years, but all the same, I find it very unlikely that it has changed so much that such a thing could take place without anyone's hearing of it.

BROTHER COMO: I often get the impression that she contradicts herself. When you ask her questions, she gets flustered, cuts her answers short, and ends up getting impatient, saying this is not the Inquisition.

SETTIMIA: All that will come to a bad end! I have had bad fortune all my life, Brother Como! A careless, erratic husband (may God have mercy on his soul!) who did me great harm. It would have taken precious little to remain in his father's good graces. If he had flattered his father's pride a little instead of constantly provoking his hostility, he could have convinced him to pay his debts and do something for Astolphe. But he had a tumultuous and impetuous character, like his son. He made a point to get himself cast out of his father's house, and today we pay the price of his folly.

BROTHER COMO (*with a malicious and sanctimonious air*): That was a serious case . . . very serious! . . .

SETTIMIA: What case do you mean?

BROTHER COMO: Ah! Your Ladyship must already know what I refer to. As for me, I only know what people have told me. Back then I did not have the honor of being Your Ladyship's confessor. (*Snickers vulgarly.*)

SETTIMIA: Brother Como, at times you joke strangely, I must say.

BROTHER COMO: I fail to see how the joke could hurt Your Ladyship. Prince Jules was a great sinner, and Your Ladyship was the most beautiful woman of her time . . . It is still obvious that your renown was well deserved. As for Your Ladyship's virtue, it was what it has always been. That must have stirred up great resentment in the prince's vindictive soul. Your father-in-law's conduct must have destroyed all filial respect in the mind of your husband, Count Octave. When such events occur in households, and we know, alas! they do occur all too often, it is hard for the families not to fall into complete disarray.

SETTIMIA: Brother Como, since you have heard about this horrible affair, let me assure you that I would not have needed my husband's help to repulse such hateful advances. It was up to me to defend myself and keep a distance. I did just that. But it was for him to appear unaware of anything, in order to avoid causing a scandal and getting disinherited by his father. What came of it? Astolphe, raised in aristocratic affluence, could not get used to poverty. In just a few years he squandered his paltry inheritance. And now he lives in boredom and privation in the remote countryside, with a mother who can only cry over his folly, and a wife incapable of making him any wiser. It is all sad, very sad!

BROTHER COMO: Well, a wonderful and happy ending is still possible! If the young Gabriel of Bramante dies before Astolphe, Astolphe inherits the title and fortune of his grandfather.

SETTIMIA: Ah! as long as the prince lives, he will find a way to prevent that. If he had to remarry at his age, he would go that far. If he had to pretend to have a child from the marriage, he would be shameless enough to do so.

BROTHER COMO: Who would believe it?

SETTIMIA: We live in poverty, while he is all-powerful!

BROTHER COMO: But do you know what people are saying? Something I hardly dare tell you, for fear of giving you false hope.

BARBE: What then? Tell us, Brother Como!

BROTHER COMO: Well, I have heard tell that young Gabriel is dead.

SETTIMIA: Mother of God in heaven! If only it were so! And Astolphe knows nothing! . . . He never concerns himself with what should most interest him.

BROTHER COMO: Oh! Let us not rejoice yet! The old prince flatly denies it. He says that his grandson is traveling abroad, and backs it up with letters that he receives from time to time.

SETTIMIA: But maybe the letters are forged!

BROTHER COMO: Maybe! But not enough time has passed since the young man's disappearance for us to justify the claim.

BARBE: The young man disappeared?

BROTHER COMO: He was raised in the country, far from all eyes. Since he was born of a sickly father who died prematurely, it was believed he would be fragile and destined for a similar fate. But when he appeared in Florence last year, people saw a handsome boy with a good constitution. And though he was delicate and svelte like his father, he was fresh as a rose, quick, bold, a rather bad type, gadding about, and even with Astolphe, who latched onto him as a friend, and who actually did not influence his behavior enough to incur the wrath of his grandfather. (*Settimia makes a gesture of surprise.*) We knew nothing of all that. Astolphe had the shrewdness to keep it to himself, which would lead us to believe he is not so foolish as we think.

SETTIMIA (*proudly*): Brother Como, Astolphe would not have been so calculating! Astolphe is frankness itself!

BROTHER COMO: And yet his marriage leaves you with some doubts about his truthfulness. But let us put that aside.

SETTIMIA: Yes, indeed, tell me what you know. Who told you all this?

BROTHER COMO: One of the brothers in our cloister, who arrived from Tuscany and talked to me this morning.

SETTIMIA: Imagine that! And we know nothing of what is going on! And so?

BROTHER COMO: The young prince, after living in grand style in the city, disappeared one fine night. Some say he abducted a woman; others that he himself was abducted by order of his grandfather and locked up in some castle until he overcomes his penchant for debauchery. Still others think that he received a thrust in some tavern which sent him off to his maker, and that old Jules is hiding his death so that you will not celebrate so soon, and to put off as long as possible the moment when the younger branch of the family will prevail. There you have what I heard; but do not put too much faith in it, because it might be entirely untrue.

SETTIMIA: But there could be some truth in all that. We absolutely must find out. Ah, my God! and Astolphe who does nothing! . . . He must leave immediately for Florence.

Scene 2

Astolphe, the characters from the previous scene.

BROTHER COMO: You could not have come at a better time; we were speaking of you.

ASTOLPHE (*curtly*): I am greatly flattered. Mother, how are you today?[26]

SETTIMIA: Ah! My son! I feel revived. And if I could believe what has been reported to Brother Como, I would be cured once and for all.

ASTOLPHE: Brother Como may be a great doctor, but I would trust him very little with our health, and even less with our personal concerns.

BROTHER COMO: I do not understand . . .

ASTOLPHE: Very well. I shall make myself clear, but not here.

SETTIMIA (*entirely preoccupied and not paying attention to what Astolphe says*): Astolphe, listen now! He says that the heir of the elder branch of the family has disappeared and is believed dead.

ASTOLPHE: That is false. He is in England, where he is completing his education. I recently received a letter from him.

---

[26] As a sign of respect for one's elders, particularly in families of high rank, children often used *vous* to address their parents. Astolphe uses *vous* with Settimia, who addresses her son using *tu*.

SETTIMIA (*chagrined and disappointed*): Is that true?

BARBE: Alas!

BROTHER COMO: Farewell to all our dreams!

ASTOLPHE: Pious sentiments! A charitable funeral oration! Mother, if that is how Brother Como teaches Christian charity, then permit me to reject his creed. My cousin is a charming boy, full of heart and soul. He has done me favors. I respect and love him, and if he should die, no one would miss him more profoundly than I.

BROTHER COMO (*shrewdly*): How touching and profound!

ASTOLPHE: Save your praise for those who think it is worth something.

SETTIMIA: Astolphe, is it possible? You were friendly with that young man and never told us?

ASTOLPHE: Dear Mother, it is not my fault if I cannot always speak candidly. You have surrounded yourself with individuals who force me to keep things inside. But today I hold nothing back, starting right now. That monk has to leave here and never come back.

SETTIMIA: Good heavens! What am I hearing? My son speaking that way to my confessor!

ASTOLPHE: It is not to him, dear Mother, that I wish to speak, it is to you . . . I insist that you send him away immediately.

SETTIMIA: Dear Jesus, do you hear him? This ungodly son of mine giving his mother orders!

ASTOLPHE: You are right, I should not have addressed myself to you, dear lady. You do not and cannot know . . . what I would rather not say. But this man understands me. (*To Brother Como.*) So I speak to you because I must. Get out, now.

BROTHER COMO: I see that you are in a state of blind, raging madness. I am duty-bound not to resist, for that would cause you to sin . . . I shall retire in all humility. I leave to God the task of enlightening you. Time and circumstances will prove that I am innocent of whatever accusations it pleases you to make.

SETTIMIA: I will not stand for my confessor being insulted and cast out this way, before my very eyes, under my own roof. You, Astolphe, are the one who must leave this room and not return unless it is to ask forgiveness for your wrongs.

ASTOLPHE: I shall ask your forgiveness, Mother, on my knees if you want. But first I am going to throw this monk out the window.[27]

---

[27] Though Brother Como is a friar, Astolphe uses the word "monk" here as a generic term, which the French language allows. A monk lived in a monastery, whereas a friar took the vows of poverty and chastity to live according to monastic principles in the secular world. Friars' impeccable reputation for humility and charity came into question as they began collecting ever larger sums of money, which they used for the upkeep of lavish gifts they received from the wealthy. See Bishop 164–71.

Brother Como, who has reassumed his haughty demeanor, pales and backs up to the door. Settimia falls on a chair ready to faint.

BARBE (*rubs Settimia's hands*): Ave Maria! What a scandal! Lord, have pity on us! . . .

BROTHER COMO: Young man! May heaven enlighten you!

Astolphe gestures menacingly. Brother Como flees.

Scene 3

Settimia, Barbe, Astolphe.

ASTOLPHE (*approaches his mother*): For my sake, Mother, come to your senses. I would have wished for it all to take place a bit less abruptly and certainly not in your presence. That is how I had vowed it would happen, but he went too far. The sanctimonious arrogance of that man made me lose the little patience I possess.

Settimia cries.

BARBE: And what did that man do, to put you in such a fury?

ASTOLPHE: Barbe, this is no concern of yours. Leave me alone with my mother.

BARBE: So you are going to chase me from the house, too?

ASTOLPHE (*takes her arm and leads her to the door*): Go say your prayers, my good woman, and take your ill humor with you. There is already enough bad feeling in here.

Barbe exits muttering.

Scene 4

Astolphe, Settimia.

SETTIMIA (*sobs*): Now will you tell me, you monstrous child, why you behave this way?

ASTOLPHE: Mother, I beg you not to ask me. You know I am only too indulgent by nature, not spiteful or suspicious. Please have the love and respect to believe me: I had the best of reasons not to tolerate another hour of that monk's presence.

SETTIMIA: Am I supposed to bow to your personal judgment, without even knowing why you deprive me of a saintly man who has been at my side and guided my conscience for ten years? Astolphe, this goes beyond the bounds of tyranny.

ASTOLPHE: You want me to tell you? Very well, I shall, to put an end to your regrets and show you in what sort of hands you put your will and the secrets of your soul. That good monk was hounding my wife with his vile entreaties.

SETTIMIA: Your wife is ungodly. He was trying to lead her to Christian duty, and I was the one who encouraged him.

ASTOLPHE: Oh, Mother! You do not, you cannot understand . . . your pure soul prevents you from suspecting such things! . . . That wretch burned with shameful desires for Gabrielle, and he dared tell her so.

SETTIMIA: Gabrielle said that? Then it is slander. Such a thing is impossible. I do not believe it; I shall never believe it.

ASTOLPHE: Gabrielle, commit slander? Mother, you cannot mean that!

SETTIMIA: I believe it! I believe it so much that I intend to unmask her in Brother Como's presence.

ASTOLPHE: You would not do such a thing, Mother; no, you could not!

SETTIMIA: I shall! We will see if she stands by her lies when confronted by the saintly man in my presence.

ASTOLPHE: Her lies? Am I having a bad dream? Is it Gabrielle my mother speaks of in such terms? What is happening in the family I returned to, full of trust and devotion, looking for respect and happiness?

SETTIMIA: Happiness! To know happiness, one must give it to others. You and your wife do nothing but give me pain.

ASTOLPHE: What! If it is I whom you accuse, Mother, then I can only bow my head and cry, although in truth

I do not feel guilty. But Gabrielle! What could be the crimes of that sweet, angelic creature?

SETTIMIA: Ah! You wish me to tell you? Very well! I wish it too, because I have suffered in silence long enough, carrying what feels like a mountain of pain and loathing in my heart. I hate your Gabrielle. I hate her for goading you on and helping you every day to deceive me by passing herself off as a girl of good family and a rich heiress, when she is nothing but a schemer with no name, no fortune, no family, no reputation, and what is more, no religion! I hate her because she ruins you by enticing you to spend foolishly, to revolt against me, to hate the people who surround me and are dear to me . . . I hate her because you prefer her to me; because at the slightest disagreement between the two of us, you take her side, despite the love and respect you owe me. I hate her . . .

ASTOLPHE: Enough, Mother, have mercy; say no more! You hate her because I love her. There is no more to say.

SETTIMIA (*cries*): Very well, then, yes! I hate her because you love her, and you no longer love me because I hate her. We have reached that point. How do you expect me to accept your preference for her? What! The child who owes me the light of day, whom I nursed at my breast, rocked on my lap, the young man I worked so hard to raise, for whom I sacrificed myself, whose every fault I forgave; the child who condemned me to insomnia, worries, suffering of all kinds, who, with the slightest gesture of repentance and affection, has always received unlimited indulgence and untiring benevolence from me. That child prefers a stranger to me, a girl who turns him against me, a heartless creature who takes up all his attention, all his consideration, who, all day long, displays a haughty attitude toward me, without bothering to notice my tears and my heartbreak, without wanting to respond to my complaints and my reproaches, impassive in her hypocritical pride, whose insolently polite stare seems to say at every moment: Your rebukes, your weeping, your threats are in vain; I am the one he loves, I am the one he respects, I am the one he fears! One word from my lips, one look from my eyes, will make him fall at my feet and follow me, even if he had to abandon you on your deathbed, even if he had to walk over your dead body to come to me. Good God! Good God! And he wonders why I hate her, and he expects me to love her! *(Sobs.)*

ASTOLPHE *(who has listened in utter silence, arms crossed over his chest)*: O jealousy of woman! Unquenchable thirst for control! Could your abominable influence have contaminated the purest and most sacred feelings of nature! O jealousy! I thought only base and vindictive souls could feel your torments. I have seen you triumph in the immoral speech of courtesans. In the brutal ardor of debauchery, I myself struggled against your ferocious instincts, which demeaned me in my own eyes. Sometimes, O jealousy! I saw you poison the dignity of a conjugal union, and contaminate sacred love with shameful discord, with ridiculous quarrels that demean both their perpetrators and their innocent victims alike! But never would I have thought that you would dare stir up turmoil in the august sanctuary of the family, between a mother and her children (a sacred link that Providence seems to have purified and ennobled even in the beast)! O wretched instinct; pathetic need to suffer and to make others suffer! Is it possible that I find you in my own mother's heart! (*Puts his face in his hands and conceals his tears.*)

SETTIMIA (*wipes her eyes and stands*): My son, this is a cruel lesson for me! I do not know how proper it is for a son to give his mother such a rebuke, but wherever it comes from, I accept it as a trial sent from God. If I deserved it from you, it is a punishment sufficient to absolve me of all the wrongs for which you could reproach me. (*Tries to leave.*)

ASTOLPHE (*holds her back*): Not like this, Mother, do not go away like this. You feel too much pain, and so do I!

SETTIMIA: Let me retire to my chapel, Astolphe. I need to be alone and ask God if I must now play the role of an outraged mother or a fearful and repentant slave. (*Exits.*)

Scene 5

Astolphe alone, then Gabrielle.

ASTOLPHE: Pride! All women are your victims, all love is your prey! . . . Except you, except your love, my Gabrielle! . . . Oh, my only joy, oh, the only generous and truly noble being I have met on earth!

GABRIELLE (*embraces him*): My love, I heard everything. I was sitting on the bench below the window. I now know what my presence in the family has brought about. I know that I am a subject of scandal, a source of conflict, an object of hatred.

ASTOLPHE: O my sister! My wife![28] From the moment I began loving you, I believed I could never be unhappy again! And to think she is my mother! . . .

GABRIELLE: Do not blame her, my beloved; she is old, she is a woman! She cannot overcome her prejudices; she cannot repress her instincts. Do not fight the inevitable.

---

[28] In the late eighteenth-century and early nineteenth centuries, incest was a recurrent theme in works of French literature. These works were more about the danger, titillation, or avoidance of incest than its actual consummation. Characters in French novels of the time, including several novels by George Sand, occasionally address their lovers affectionately as "sister," "mother," or "my child." But characters who were in fact related by blood did not get married (see Pasco). Though Astolphe's use of the term "sister" may express his deep bond with Gabrielle, it could also suggest that something is fundamentally wrong or impossible about their relationship, especially since they are first cousins.

I had foreseen it from the first day, and not for the world would I have told you before now that this would happen. Bad things always happen soon enough.

ASTOLPHE: Oh, Gabrielle! You heard her diatribe against you! . . . If anyone else but my mother had said one hundredth of what—

GABRIELLE: Be calm! I do not take offense at her criticism. I can bear it with resignation and patience. Have I not your love to compensate for all adversity? As long as you find in mine the strength to endure all the hardships that arise from our predicament . . .

ASTOLPHE: I can endure anything, except to see you degraded and persecuted.

GABRIELLE: Such insults do not disturb me. You see, Astolphe, you made me a woman again, but I have not altogether renounced being a man. (Even though I have assumed the clothing and occupations of my sex, I have conserved the inner tendency to noble-mindedness, the calm strength a male upbringing developed and cultivated within me.) still feel I am something more than a woman, and no woman can stir me to loathing, resentment, or anger. Perhaps it is pride, but I feel it would be lowering myself to get upset over petty domestic quarrels.

ASTOLPHE: Oh! Keep that pride; it is quite legitimate . . . Adorable being! You alone are greater than all the members of your sex combined. Credit your upbringing if you wish, but I think the praise goes to your nature. I do not think you needed a singular fate, an existence outside all known laws in order to be divine creation's masterpiece. You were born endowed with all faculties, all virtues, all graces, and you are misunderstood! You are vilified!

GABRIELLE: What does it matter to you? Let the storms pass. Love's holy protection keeps us safe. Besides, I will try to ward them off. Perhaps I have been wrong. I could have shown more regard for strict rules of conduct that are really harmless in themselves. If our hunting parties cause displeasure, I can forgo them. If our ideas on religious tolerance cause dismay, we can remain silent on the subject. If I am regarded as too elegant and useless, I can dress more simply and take on more household chores.

ASTOLPHE: But that is precisely what I cannot tolerate. I would be a scoundrel if I forgot what you sacrificed for me by wearing the clothes of your sex and giving up the freedom, the active life, the noble occupations of the mind that you enjoyed and were used to. Give up your horse? Alas! It is the only exercise that has saved your health from the decline that was brought on by the change in your ways and that was beginning to worry me. Dress more simply? Your dress is already so modest! And a bit of finery does so bring out your beauty! As a young man, you loved rich clothes, and you gave our capricious fashions a grace and poetry that none of us could imitate. You need the love of beauty and sense of elegance to live, Gabrielle. You would suffocate under the heavy hoops and starched collars of Lady Barbe. Housework would ruin your beautiful hands, whose touch on my forehead drives away all my cares and dispels all my troubles. Besides, what would happen to your mind's noble thoughts and poetic inspirations if you were mired in tedious details and selfish, stingy frugality? Those poor women boast of their drudgery out of pride, and twenty times a day they betray the immense dissatisfaction and boredom of their lives. As for hiding your generous sentiments and submitting to the constraints of intolerance, you would try in vain. Never will your heart grow cold, never will you be able to abandon your steadfast allegiance to the truth. You could not prevent the flashes of your unflinching indignation from shining through the darkness that fanaticism would try to spread over your soul. Besides, if all our trials are not beyond your own strength, I feel that they are beyond mine. I could not see you being oppressed without protesting vehemently. You have suffered so much already; you have sacrificed yourself quite enough for my sake.

GABRIELLE: I have not suffered. I have not immolated myself in the least. I merely trusted you. Well do you know that my spirit was strong enough to accept the first few days' small privations that came with the change in ways that you refer to. There were things I abhorred more, and I had more serious fears. You dispelled them all. As a woman I have not fallen from the rank where your friendship placed me as a man. I have not ceased to be your brother and friend while becoming your companion and beloved. Have you not made concessions for me, too? Have you not changed your life for me?

ASTOLPHE: Oh! You praise me for my sacrifices! I gave up a life of exhausting chaos, a life of debauchery I increasingly loathed, in exchange for a sublime love and ideal joys! Yet you praise me for the respect and veneration I have for you! I had the best of friends in you. Then one night God performed a miracle and changed you into an adorable mistress and I only loved you more. Is that so charitable and honorable of me?

GABRIELLE: Dear Astolphe, I see that you are calm again. Go kiss and reassure your mother, or let me speak to her for both of us. I will appease her; I will overcome her prejudices. My sincerity will reach her, I am sure of it. It is impossible for her not to be loving and generous; she is your mother! . . .

ASTOLPHE: Dear angel! Yes, I am calm. As soon as I am near you, every storm is dispelled, and heavenly peace descends upon my soul. I shall go find my mother, show her respect and submission, which is all she asks. After that, let us leave this place, because I know the harm is irreparable! I know my mother, I know women.(You do not know them, you who are not half man, half woman, as you believe, but rather an angel in human form) Your attempt to use patience and virtue would be futile. They would not find it convincing, and even if they did, your superiority would humiliate them further and increase their hostility. You know well that when someone is wronged, the guilty party does not forgive the innocent one. It is an immutable law of human pride. Especially feminine pride, which has no knowledge of reason as a recourse and no intellectual strength to keep pride in check. My mother's pride comes before all else. She was always a model of domestic virtues. Believe me, they are paltry virtues when not inspired by love or devotion. Imbued for so long with the sense of her own important role in the family, and the praiseworthy manner in which she fulfilled her duty, she cares much more about holding on to her prerogatives than about giving happiness to those around her. People like her will readily spend the night mending your breeches, and then, with one word, break your heart, thinking that the trouble they took to do you a favor gives them the right to make you suffer.

GABRIELLE: Astolphe! You judge your mother so coldly and harshly. Alas! I see that the best of men have neither deep love nor complete respect for women. They were right to teach me so carefully during my childhood that this sex plays the most abject and unhappy role on earth!

ASTOLPHE: Oh, beloved! Only my love for you gives me the courage to judge my mother so harshly. Is it fair of you to reproach me for it? Have I given you any cause to deplore so grievously the womanly role I restored to you?

GABRIELLE (*embraces him warmly*): No, dear Astolphe, never! I do not think of myself when I speak so freely of things that are not my business. But do let me speak more on your mother's behalf. Do not cast her into despair. Do not leave her because of me.

ASTOLPHE: If I stay here a day longer, she will give me no choice but to leave. You forget, my dear Gabrielle, that where she is concerned, you are in a delicate position. She will never be satisfied, because you cannot tell her what she wants most to know: your past, your family, your future.

GABRIELLE: You are right. Especially my future, who can predict it? What an endless labyrinth you have got yourself into with me!

ASTOLPHE: Do we need a way out? Let us go on this way all our lives, without worrying about achieving fortune and honors. Are we not together as we take this strange and delightful journey that only death will end? Are you not mine forever? Well then, what need have we to be rich and call ourselves the Prince of Bramante? My little prince, keep your title, keep your inheritance. I do not want it at any price. And if, in his tortuous little brain, old Jules hatches some new secret plan for stripping them from you, then console yourself with being no more than a woman, poor and unknown to the world, but rich in my love and glorious in my eyes.

GABRIELLE: Do you fear that will not be enough for me?

ASTOLPHE (*clasps her in his arms*): No, in truth! I have no such fear. I feel in my heart how much you love me.

ACT 4

In a small country house, secluded deep in
the mountains. A very simple room arranged
with taste; some flowers, books, and
musical instruments.

Scene 1

GABRIELLE (*alone; sketches, stops now and then to look out
the window*): Marc might come back today. If only he
could arrive before Astolphe returns from his walk. I
should like to speak with him alone and learn the whole
truth. With each passing day, our situation worries me
more. For I sense in Astolphe the beginnings of a strange
inner turmoil . . . I might be mistaken. But what could
be the reason for his sadness? Little by little, unhappiness crept into our lives. First it was like a dullness that
stole into our souls, then a sickness that made us deliri-
ous. Now it is like an all-consuming agony. Alas! Is love
truly so delicate a flame that the slightest disrespect for its
sacredness causes it to vanish and return to the heavens?

Astolphe! Astolphe! How badly you have treated me. You have made bleed most cruelly this heart that was and always will be faithful to you! I have forgiven you all. May God forgive you! But it is a great crime to have tarnished such love with mistrust and suspicion. And now you pay the price, for this love has been weakened by its very violence. Because your extreme jealousy ignited too often that inner flame, you now feel it waning more each day. Unhappy friend! In vain do I beseech you to forget the harm you did us both, for it is no longer within your power! Your soul has lost the flower of its generous youth. It is weighed down by a hidden remorse that yet fails to prevent further misdeeds. Ah! No doubt love offers a sanctuary we can no longer return to once we have taken a single step outside its boundaries, and the barrier that separated us from harm can no longer be raised up again. Error follows upon error, outrage upon outrage, bitterness grows like a torrent past broken dams . . . What will be the end to this havoc? Can even my own love fall prey? Will it succumb to weariness, tears, consuming worries? It still seems strong as ever to me, and unshaken by suffering. Astolphe has been foolish but not guilty. His misdeeds have been almost involuntary, and his repentance has always wiped the slate clean. But if his misdeeds became more serious, if he were coldly to insult me by imposing on me this confinement, which I accept devotedly to give in to his wishes . . . could I look at him with the same eyes? Could I love him with the same tenderness? . . . Has not his erratic behavior already diminished my ardor for him? . . . But Astolphe could never become coldhearted or go that much astray! His is a noble soul, unselfish, heroically generous. His faults are so minor compared with his virtues! . . . Alas! There was a time when he had no faults at all! . . . Oh Astolphe! How you hurt me when you destroyed my belief in your perfection. (*Knock on the door.*) Who is here? Perhaps it is Marc.

Scene 2

Marc, Gabrielle.

MARC (*in boots, holds a riding crop*): I come back to you a bit tired, Signora,[29] but I would not rest a single moment until I could tell you exactly what transpired.

GABRIELLE: Well, my old friend, how was my grandfather when you left?

MARC: Somewhat better than when I arrived. But still very ill. He could probably last another three months.

---

[29] "Signora" appears in the French text, even though Gabrielle and Faustina are addressed as "Madame" (in English, "Madam") elsewhere in the original. We cannot be certain whether this difference is Sand's oversight or intended. Even if an oversight, it's interesting when compared with her use of Italian terms of address in many of her other works set in Italy.

GABRIELLE: Was he quite angry that I did not go myself to see how he was?

MARC: A little. I told him, just as we agreed, that Your Lordship sprained your ankle at the hunt and most regretfully had to stay in bed.

GABRIELLE: No doubt he asked where I was?

MARC: Indeed. I replied that you were still in Cosenza. Whereupon he said, "He is in Cosenza this year the way he was in Palermo last year, and at that time he was in Palermo the way he was in Genoa the previous year." I managed to look very surprised, and since he thinks I am perfectly dull-witted (as he always puts it), he was completely duped by my good faith. "How is it," he asked, "that you do not know where he has been for three years?" "Your Highness well knows," I answered, "that I have been keeping up the palace that my lord Gabriel occupies in Florence. Around the feast of Saint Hubert, His Lordship departs for the hunt with some or other of his friends, and he brings along only his grooms and page. I offer to go with him, but he says, 'You are too old to run after deer, my poor Marc; you are only good for guarding the house.' And the truth is . . ." Then my lord interrupted me: "I have heard that he took none of his servants, and that he is always left alone. And it has been noticed that Astolphe Bramante always leaves Florence around the same time." When I saw the prince so well informed, I almost lost my composure. But he considers me so simple-minded that he did not take notice, and he turned toward your tutor, Father Chiavari, and said, "Father, all this hardly surprises me. It is quite obvious that love is behind all these machinations. But it is harder on them to make things work out than it is on me to see them engage in this ridiculous intrigue."

GABRIELLE: And what was Father Chiavari's reply?

MARC: He lowered his eyes and sighed, "A woman . . ."

GABRIELLE: Go on.

MARC: ". . . will always be a woman!" His Highness was playing with your little dog and appeared to be laughing to himself, which frightened me a little, because, whenever the Prince contemplates something sinister, he tends to smile and make poor Mosca yelp by pulling on his ears.

GABRIELLE: And what did he instruct you to tell me?

MARC: He spoke rather harshly . . .

GABRIELLE: Repeat it word for word.

MARC: "You tell your Lord Gabriel that whatever pleasure he takes in the hunt, or however he has sprained his foot, that he has one week to come here and receive my orders. He has little time to lose if he wants to see me alive, and expects me to confer on him his legal title and inheritance, which could successfully be contested upon my death."

GABRIELLE: What did he mean? Does he think Astolphe plans to raise a scandal to claim his rights?

MARC: He thinks Lord Astolphe has that very thing in mind, and I do too, if I dared tell Your Lordship what I think . . .

GABRIELLE: You think nothing, Marc.

MARC: My lord wishes me to keep silent. Nonetheless, it is my duty to say what I know. Last summer Lord Astolphe had your nanny brought to Florence. He offered her money if she would testify in court what she knows, including the events surrounding your birth . . .

GABRIELLE: You were misinformed, Marc. That never happened.

MARC: The nanny herself told me during my recent stay at the Bramante castle, and showed me a beautiful full purse that Lord Astolphe gave her just to keep his offer quiet, because she obstinately denied to him that she had nursed a female child.

GABRIELLE: The nanny sells herself to the highest bidder; because she undoubtedly told this to my grandfather.

MARC: I am afraid so.

GABRIELLE: What does it matter? Astolphe's intention was surely to test my servants' loyalty.

MARC: Whatever Lord Astolphe's intentions, I believe that the time has come for Your Lordship to obey his grandfather's wishes. All the more so because as I was leaving the castle, the priest furtively approached me and whispered in my ear, "Tell Gabriel, from a true friend, that he must not be unwise. He must go to his grandfather and obey or else feign to obey blindly. If he refuses to follow orders, he must hide well enough to avoid an ambush. He must know that his life is at stake. One false step, and the Prince will stop at nothing if the family's honor is compromised." Those are the exact words of your tutor, and he is sincerely devoted to you, my lord.

GABRIELLE: I believe it. I shall not ignore this warning. Now, go rest, my dear Marc. You need it badly.

MARC: Yes indeed! Perhaps, after I have rested, I will remember something else, other words I cannot recall right now. (*Starts to leave.*)

GABRIELLE (*calls him back*): Listen, Marc: if my husband questions you, be careful not to mention the nanny . . .

MARC: I will be most careful, my lord!

GABRIELLE: Then learn to stop calling me that. When we are here and I am clothed as a woman, all that recalls my other sex infuriates Astolphe.

MARC: Indeed! Dear God, I know that only too well! But what can I do? No sooner do I learn to call Your Lordship madam then off we go to Florence and you don your male attire. I still have "madam" on my lips, and just when I begin to say "my lord," Your Lordship is back in a dress and hair combs. (*Exits.*)

Scene 3

GABRIELLE: This story about the nanny is a calumny. It is a new ruse of my grandfather's to turn me against

Astolphe. He must have paid that woman to tell such a tale to my poor Marc, certain that Marc would inform me. Oh! No, Astolphe, no, you would never wrong me that way! You are the one who insisted that I not reveal the scheme that forces me to deny you officially the title you refuse to assume and the wealth I restore to you in secret. You are the one who, with all the authority granted by a generous love, forbade me to make my sex public and renounce the usurped rights conferred on me by unjust laws. Had you the slightest regret, you would have scrupled to let me know, because you can be quite certain I would not have hesitated to give them up. In those days, I did not think you ever possibly could make me suffer. My eyes were closed and my trust complete! . . . But now, I confess I am reluctant to renounce being a man when I wish; because I have not been happy for long in this other disguise, which has become our mutual torment. But if that were the only way to please you, would I hesitate for a moment? Oh! You have no cause to doubt, Astolphe. You would not scheme behind my back to make me do all that I would do willingly at your request. You, set a trap for me? You, plot against me? No, no, never! . . . Here he is, back from his walk. I shall not even bring it up, so little reassurance do I need of his frankness and generosity.

Scene 4

Astolphe, Gabrielle.

ASTOLPHE: Well, dearest Gabrielle, your old servant has returned. I just saw his horse in the courtyard. What news has he brought you from Bramante?

GABRIELLE: He believes our grandfather will die soon. But in my opinion, the old man still has a good deal of time left. He is not one to die so readily. But do we want his death? However much he wronged us both (and I do think that the worst wrongs were done to the one he seemed to favor at the expense of the other), let us not hasten with ungodly wishes the supreme instant when he will face harsh judgment for his children's fate. May he find in the skies above a judge as charitable as we are. Do you not agree, Astolphe? Are you listening?

ASTOLPHE: Quite right, Gabrielle; you become more a thinker every day. You reason from morning to night like a scholar from Crusca.[30] Could you not be a woman for at least three months of the year?

GABRIELLE (*smiles*): Those three months were a long time ago, Astolphe. The first time, the term was indeed three months, but the second time it was six. I fear that

---

[30] Like a professor of philosophy.

next year, the term will last a whole twelve months, despite our agreement. If I must be a woman so often these days, then give me the time to get used to it. Earlier on, you were not so difficult with me, and it did not occur to me soon enough to shed my schoolboy's language. You should have warned me from the first day you loved me, that the time would come when I would have to change who I am to keep your love!

ASTOLPHE: That reproach is unfair, Gabrielle! But even if it were true, have I not also changed to deserve and keep the affection of your heart?

GABRIELLE: You are right, my dear angel, and I am glad to be wrong. I will try to adjust.

ASTOLPHE (*walks with a worried look, then stops and looks at Gabrielle with tenderness*): Poor Gabrielle! How your endless deference grieves me.

GABRIELLE (*extends her hand*): Why? It does not try me as you think.

ASTOLPHE (*presses Gabrielle's hand to his lips for a long time, then paces, agitated*): I know! You are strong! No one can wound your pride. The storms that rage in others' souls cannot dim the bright, beautiful sky where your thoughts expand, free and proud! One could easily chain your arms, whose delicate beauty could not be destroyed by a Spartan education. But your soul is independent as the birds that fly, as the ocean waves. How well do I know that all the powers of the universe combined could not bend it!

GABRIELLE: Above all the forces of matter, there is a divine force that has always chained me to you: it is love. My pride does not rise above that power. This too you well know.

ASTOLPHE (*stops her*): Oh, you speak truly, my beloved! But have I lost any trace of that sublime love that was once ever eager to grant me the slightest wish?

GABRIELLE (*tenderly*): Why would you have lost it?

ASTOLPHE: You do not remember, generous heart, oh true heart of a man! (*Clasps her in his arms.*)

GABRIELLE: See, my friend, how your greatest compliment is to assign me the qualities of your sex. And yet, how you often would like me to lower myself to the weakness of my own! So be consistent!

ASTOLPHE (*embraces her*): Do I know what I want? To the devil with being consistent! I love you passionately!

GABRIELLE: Dear Astolphe!

ASTOLPHE (*falls to his knees*): So you still love me?

GABRIELLE: You know that I do.

ASTOLPHE: As you did before?

GABRIELLE: Not as before, but as much, maybe more.

ASTOLPHE: Why not as before? You refused me nothing then!

GABRIELLE: And what do I refuse you now?

ASTOLPHE: There is yet something you will refuse me if I chance to ask you.

GABRIELLE: Ah! Schemer! You want to lead me into a trap?

ASTOLPHE: Yes, I do.

GABRIELLE: Please, Astolphe, no subterfuge. When I give in to you, is it ever warily and cautiously, and with stipulations?

ASTOLPHE: Oh! You know I hate subterfuge. My soul was once so naive! It was open and trusting, like yours. But alas! I have been so guilty! As I learned to doubt myself, I came to doubt others.

GABRIELLE: Put it out of your mind as I have, and tell me.

ASTOLPHE: The time has come to return to Florence. Please agree not to go. You look away! You do not speak? Do you refuse me?

GABRIELLE (*sadly*): No, I agree, but on one condition: that you tell me the reason for your request.

ASTOLPHE: The price of your favor is too high. Do not ask me what I am ashamed to confess.

GABRIELLE: Must I try to guess, Astolphe? Is it the same reason as before? (*Astolphe nods.*) Jealousy? (*Astolphe nods again.*) What! Again! Still! Dear God, Astolphe, we are indeed ill-fated!

ASTOLPHE: Ah! Do not tell me that! Conceal the tears that roll from your eyes, do not break my heart! I feel like such a coward. Yet I lack the strength to give up what you grant me with your tear-filled eyes and broken heart! Why do you still love me, Gabrielle? Why do you not despise me! For as long as you love me, I shall demand, I shall be unreasonable, because the fear of losing you is a torment. I sense that I shall lose you, because I sense the pain that I cause you. But I am sliding down a fatal slope. I would rather tumble to the bottom all at once. Then, as soon as you despise me, I shall no longer suffer, I shall cease to exist.

GABRIELLE: O love! Then you are not a religion? You have no revelations, no laws, no prophets? You have not, then, grown stronger in men's hearts, along with knowledge and freedom? Then you are always subject to the whims of blind fate, and we have failed to find in ourselves some sort of strength or will, some virtue to avert your perils and avoid your debacle? So we shall not receive divine assistance from heaven to purify you in ourselves, to ennoble you and raise you above brute instinct, to preserve you from your own furies and make you triumph over your own madness? So you must eternally succumb, devoured by your own flames, and with our pride and selfishness we must take the purest and most divine balm ever given to us on earth and turn it into poison?

ASTOLPHE: Ah! My love, your lofty soul is always prey to illusions. You dream of an ideal love the way I once dreamed of an ideal woman. My dream came true, care-free and wayward as I am! But yours will not come true, my poor Gabrielle! You will never find a heart worthy of your own. Never will you be satisfied with the love you inspire, because never has a cult been worthy of your divinity. If men still do not know the true homage that pleases God, how do you expect them to find on earth that grain of pure incense whose perfume has still not risen to heaven? So come down from the empyrean height where you boldly strive to fly, and become patient under the yoke of life. Make God alone the keeper of your heart, or else consent to be loved like a mortal. Never will you encounter a lover who is not jealous of you, and that means possessive, mistrustful, unjust, despotic.

GABRIELLE: Do you believe that I dream of love in any other soul than yours?

ASTOLPHE: You should, you could. This is what makes my jealousy more understandable and less outrageous.

GABRIELLE: Alas! Indeed, love does not reason, for I can dream of a more perfect love only by imagining it in your heart. I feel that the same love in the heart of another would not move me.

ASTOLPHE: Oh! Say that to me, say it again! Repeat it to me always! Go on, flout all reason, outrage justice. Ignore the voice of heaven itself if it speaks to your soul against me. Just so long as you love me, I am willing to suffer in another life all the pain you will endure for the folly of loving me in this life.

GABRIELLE: No, I do not want to love you in blasphemous euphoria. I want to love you religiously and join you with the idea of God in my soul, with the desire for perfection. I want to heal you, strengthen your better nature, raise you up, and lift you to the height of my ideas. Promise you will try, and I in turn will give in to you, as one gives in to children who are ill. We will not go to Florence. I will remain a woman for the entire year, and if you consent to undertake the great task of converting to a belief in true love, my sadness will turn into supreme happiness.

ASTOLPHE: Yes, I consent, my dear wife, and I thank you on my knees for wishing me that. Have you now any doubt that I am less your disciple than your slave?

GABRIELLE: You have made that promise many times before. And then, instead of keeping your word, you always gave in to new fits of jealousy. It was as if, instead of being happy and calm with me in this secluded retreat where you have hidden me from all eyes, my concessions only aggravated your jealousy, and solitude only increased your sadness. And I! I was not at all happy, for I saw all my labors in vain and all my sacrifices worsen your plight. And so I missed those intervals of respite when I dressed as a man. Then, I could at least use the ample quantities of gold from my grandfather to regale you with noble diversions and poetic distractions.

🜂 ASTOLPHE: Yes, our first days in Florence or Pisa always have great charms for me. I am not made for the reclusive idleness of the countryside. Unlike you, I do not know how to absorb myself in books or lose myself in thought. Well you know that each year we come here, the tyrant condemns himself to more suffering than his victim, and the more I suffer inside, the more I wrong you. But in the hustle and bustle of society, when you are again the handsome Gabriel, sought out, admired, coddled by everyone, it is yet another kind of suffering that takes hold of me. It is a suffering less slow to build and perhaps less profound; but it is still violent, intolerable. I cannot get used to seeing other men shake your hand or casually pass their arm under yours. I do not wish to persuade myself that you are effectively a man at those times, and that your metamorphosis shields you and would allow you to sleep safely in their rooms, as you once slept under the same roof as I without troubling my sleep. I remember the strange emotion that stole through me little by little, as I lay by your side, and how much I regretted that you were not a woman. And how I came to divine what you really were, just from longing so much for you miraculously to become one. Why would others not have the same intuition, and at the sight of you not feel the inexpressible confusion that I did, despite your man's disguise? Oh! I go through unbelievable torture when Menrique brings his horse up next to yours, or when that brutal Antonio passes his heavy hand through your hair, and says in what he believes is a jocular tone, "To think I burned with love for a whole evening for those beautiful locks!" Then I imagine that he has guessed our secret and that he insolently enjoys teasing me with his crude allusions. I am overwhelmed by the same fury that flared up in me when he tried to kiss you at Ludovic's supper. And if not for the fear of giving us both away, I would have slapped him in the face.

GABRIELLE: How can you let yourself be carried away like that when you know that I abhor such familiarities even more than you do, and that I would repel them in that same manful way if they were ever to go beyond the limits of the strictest chastity?

ASTOLPHE: Though I know that, I still feel no better! And sometimes I resent you for not being cautious enough. I imagine that, to avenge yourself for all my injustices, you make sport of my anguish, and in my thoughts I insult you . . . It takes all the strength I have just to keep you from noticing it.

GABRIELLE: And then I see your strength nearly depleted, and you almost about to lose control and do something shameful and ridiculous, or unveil our dangerous secret. And I allow myself to be brought here, where despite everything you love me less. For in the calm possession of such a coveted object your love seems to dim and die out like a flame without fuel.

ASTOLPHE: I cannot deny that. God is punishing my lack of faith. But I know I do not love you less, for the slightest worry kindles new flames of mad furor. Then, when everything is calm, I am seized with a hideous anxiety even when by your side. When you bless me, I feel that you hate me. At night, I hold you in my arms and dream that another possesses you. Oh! My beloved, have pity on me. I confess my despair; do not despise me. Make this curse go away, make me love you the way you wish to be loved!

GABRIELLE: Then what are we to do? You get furious when I am in society, and worn out when we are together alone. Do you want some distraction for a few days? Do you want to go to Florence without me?

ASTOLPHE: Sometimes I think that will do me some good. But I know that as soon as I am there, the onset of dreams more hideous than ever will disturb my sleep. By day I manage to carry your holy image in my soul. But at nightfall I picture you here with a rival.

GABRIELLE: What! You distrust me that much? Lock me up in some underground dungeon, order Marc to pass me my meals through a grating, take the keys with you, wall up the door—then will you be at peace?

ASTOLPHE: No! A man will pass by and look at you through the grating, and the mere sight of you will make him happier than I who cannot see you.

GABRIELLE: You see that jealousy is not cured by such vulgar methods. The more one gives in to it, the more it grows; only will can cure it. Undertake this healing as one undertakes the study of philosophy. Try to control your passion.

ASTOLPHE: But where did you get the strength to control yours and bend it to your will? You are not jealous of me. So do you love me only by the exercise of your reason or virtue?

GABRIELLE: Good heavens! What would become of us if I gave you the trouble you give me? Poor Astolphe! I have kept such an urge from invading my soul, though you know I have sometimes felt it! But your example led me to reflect seriously, and I swore to myself not to be like you! But what is the matter? You turn so pale!

ASTOLPHE (*looks out the window*): Look, Gabrielle! Who enters the courtyard? Look!

GABRIELLE (*indifferently*): I hear galloping. (*She looks at the courtyard.*) It appears to be Antonio! Yes, it is he. As if he heard you praise him, and with his usual good timing, decided to appear.

ASTOLPHE (*agitated*): You find it very easy to joke . . . But what brings him here? And how did he find out our retreat?

GABRIELLE: How would I know any more than you do?

ASTOLPHE (*increasingly agitated*): My God! What might I not know!

GABRIELLE (*reproachfully*): Oh! Astolphe! . . .

ASTOLPHE (*barely contains his fury*): Did you not try just a moment ago to convince me to stay in Florence by myself? Maybe Antonio has come a day too soon. One can mistake what day and time it is when one has a bad memory and is very impatient . . .

GABRIELLE: Not again! Oh! Astolphe! Already your promises forgotten! Already my submission repaid with insult!

ASTOLPE (*bitterly*): A show of anger is the only ploy left when one has tripped up! I advise you to heap insults upon me, then maybe I shall be stupid enough to ask your forgiveness. I have done it so many times before!

GABRIELLE (*raises her hand vehemently toward the sky*): My God! Great God! Give me the strength to persevere! (*Exits*).

Astolphe follows her, locks her in her room, and puts the key in his pocket.

Scene 5

Marc, Astolphe.

MARC: Lord Astolphe, Lord Antonio wishes to see you. I told him you were not here, that you had never been here, that I had quit the service of my master, but it was no use . . . What lies I told! . . . He claimed that he saw you in the park and that for an hour he circled the moat in an effort to gain entry. He finally got in and refuses to leave without seeing you first.

ASTOLPHE: I shall go meet him. You arrange this room. Get rid of everything that belongs to your mistress, and stay here until I call you! (*Aside.*) Now, then! I must steel myself, act unsuspecting. But if I find out what I dread to find out, then woe betide you, Antonio! Woe betide the two of us, Gabrielle! (*Exits.*)

Scene 6

Marc, Gabrielle.

MARC: What is wrong with him? How upset he is! Ah! My poor mistress is indeed unhappy!

GABRIELLE (*knocks from behind the door*): Marc! Let me out! Quickly! Break down this door. I want to get out.

MARC: My God! Who locked up Your Lordship? Luckily I have the double in my pocket . . . (*Opens the door.*)

GABRIELLE (*with a man's coat and hat*): Here, take this traveling bag, run to saddle my horse and yours. I want to leave here this instant.

MARC: Yes, it is the right thing to do! Lord Astolphe is most ungrateful, he only dreams of your fortune . . . How dare he lock you up! . . . Oh! Tired as I am, I shall joyfully escort you back to the castle of Bramante!

GABRIELLE: Be quiet, Marc, not a word against Astolphe. I am not going to Bramante. If you love me, then obey; go get the horses ready.

MARC: Mine is still saddled, and so is yours. Were you not to ride in the park today? I have only to bridle them.

GABRIELLE: Then run! (*Marc exits.*) You know, dear God! that resentment is not my motive and my heart has already forgiven him. But at all costs I want to rescue Astolphe from this raging affliction. I will try every means to make love triumph over jealousy. All my remedies so far have only turned to poison. But a sudden, harsh lesson might open his eyes. The more the slave bends, the heavier becomes his burden. The more a man resorts to unjust force, the more injustice becomes his necessity! He must learn the effect that tyranny has on proud souls and not think it so easy to abuse a noble love! Now he comes up the stairs with Antonio. Farewell, Astolphe! May we meet in better days! Tonight you will weep alone! May your guardian angel murmur in your ear that I still love you!

She closes her bedroom door and takes the key, then leaves through one of the salon doors, while Astolphe enters by the other, followed by Antonio.

ACT 5

Scene 1

Rome, behind the Colosseum. Night falls.

GABRIEL (*dressed as a man in black, elegant and severe, a sword at his side; he holds an open letter*): At last, the Pope grants me an audience. And in secret, just as I requested! Dear God! Protect me, and let Astolphe be at least content with his fate! I abandon my own to you, O Providence, mysterious destiny! (*Church bells ring six o'clock.*) It is time for my appointment with the holy father. Dear God! Forgive me for this last deception. You know how pure my intentions are. To dissemble is my lot, but not by my own choice, and my heart cherishes the truth! . . .

He fastens his coat, pulls his hat over his eyes, and goes toward the Colosseum. Antonio, who just left the Colosseum, bars his way.

Scene 2

Gabriel, Antonio.

ANTONIO (*masked*): I have tracked you down, watched and waited for this moment long enough. Now I have got you at last; this time you will not slip away.

Gabriel tries to pass; Antonio grabs his arm.

GABRIEL (*disengages himself*): Let me be, sir; I am not one of your party.

ANTONIO (*unmasks himself*): I am Antonio, your friend and servant. I have something to tell you and respectfully request your attention.

GABRIEL: That is quite impossible. An urgent matter awaits me. I bid you good evening.

He tries to continue; Antonio stops him again.

ANTONIO: You will not leave unless you arrange for us to meet again and tell me your whereabouts. I had the courtesy to say that I wanted to speak with you privately.

GABRIEL: Having arrived in Rome an hour ago, I shall depart immediately. Farewell.

ANTONIO: Having arrived in Rome three months ago, you will not depart until you have heard what I wish to say.

GABRIEL: Do excuse me. We have nothing particular to say to each other. I repeat; I must go immediately.

ANTONIO: I must speak to you about Astolphe. You shall listen.

GABRIEL: Well then, another time. Today it is impossible.

ANTONIO: Then tell me where you reside.

GABRIEL: I cannot.

ANTONIO: I will find out.

GABRIEL: You expect to converse with me against my will?

ANTONIO: You will be done with me sooner if you hear me right now. I will say it in two words.

GABRIEL: Well then, let us have the two words; I shall not hear more.

ANTONIO: Prince of Bramante, Your Highness is a woman. (*Aside.*) Yes, good move! Audacity is the best route.

GABRIEL (*aside*): Good heavens! Astolphe told him! (*Aloud.*) What is this foolishness? A carnival prank, I hope?

ANTONIO: Foolishness? An impertinent word! Unless you were a woman, you would not dare repeat it.

GABRIEL: (*aside*): He knows nothing! A vulgar trap! (*Aloud.*) You are a fool, as truly as I am a man.

ANTONIO: But since I do not believe it . . .

GABRIEL: You do not believe you are a fool: then I must prove it to you. (*Slaps him in the face.*)

ANTONIO: Hold it right there! My good sir! If that slap comes from the hand of a woman, I will punish it with a kiss. But if you are a man, then you must give me satisfaction.

GABRIEL (*draws his sword*): Very well.

ANTONIO (*draws his sword*): Wait! First I must tell you what I think, as I would rather you not get the wrong idea. To the best of my knowledge and belief, ever since the day I first saw you, when you were dressed as a woman for a supper at Ludovic's, I have never ceased to believe you were a woman. Your build, your face, your reserve, the sound of your voice, the way you move and walk, Astolphe's protective friendship that clearly resembles love and jealousy, all have given me reason to think that you were not disguised at Ludovic's and that you are now . . .

GABRIEL: Sir, let us cut this short; you are mad. Your absurd remarks make little difference to me. We shall fight now, so ready yourself.

ANTONIO: Oh! have a little patience, please. While there is little chance that I will lose to you, I could still die in this fight. And I would not have you walk away with the idea that I tried to court a boy; that does not suit me at all. As for myself, I wish not to believe that I am fighting with a woman, because that would put me at too great a disadvantage. To prove my case, I will tell you that I recently learned by chance that there are certain particulars concerning your family that explain quite well a lie about your sex in order to conserve an inheritance.

GABRIEL: You go too far, sir! You accuse me of lies and fraud. You insult my relations! Now you are the one who must give me satisfaction. Defend yourself.

ANTONIO: I agree to it if you are a man, for in that case, you always spurned my friendly overtures, and with such firmness that it is high time I taught you a lesson. (But since I am unsure about your sex—yes, on my honor! even as I speak, I am unsure!), we shall both fight bare-chested, please. (*Begins unbuttoning his doublet.*) I bid you follow my example.

GABRIEL: No, sir, it does not please me to catch a cold just to satisfy your impudent whim. For me to allay your suspicions by any other means than weapons would be to confess that the suspicions are somehow founded. You are well aware that to insult a man because he is neither tall nor robust is a mark of extraordinary cowardice. Keep your doubts, if you wish, until you have learned, by the way I use my sword, whether I have the right to carry it.

ANTONIO (*aside*): This is indeed the language of a man! (*Aloud.*) Are you aware that I have acquired a certain reputation as a duelist?

GABRIEL: Courage, not reputation, makes the man.

ANTONIO: But courage creates a reputation . . . You are sure about this? . . . See here! You slapped me in the face, and as a rule no apology can ever make up for that . . . However I would accept yours, since I cannot rid myself of the suspicion . . .

GABRIEL: Apology? Sir, watch what you say, and do not force me to strike you a second time . . .

ANTONIO: Oh! Oh! What outrageous presumption! . . . *En garde!* . . . Your sword is shorter than mine. Do you wish to exchange them?

GABRIEL: I am quite content with my own, thank you.

ANTONIO: Well then, we will draw lots . . .

GABRIEL: I told you I must hurry; so defend yourself! (*Attacks.*)

ANTONIO (*aside, but speaks loudly*): If the man is a woman, she will flee! . . . (*Puts up his guard.*) No . . . I will thrust lightly a few times . . . At the slightest scratch, the doublet will have to come off . . . (*The fight ensues.*) The devil! He fights like a man! This is serious now. Watch out for yourself, Prince! I am not sparing you this time!

They fight a few moments. Antonio falls, seriously wounded.

GABRIEL (*puts up his sword*): Does that satisfy you, sir?

ANTONIO: Less would have! From now on, it will not occur to me, I think, to take you for a woman! . . . Someone comes, go away, Prince! (*Tries to get up again.*)

GABRIEL: But you are badly hurt! . . . I shall help you . . .

ANTONIO: No, whoever comes will bring me help, and might harm you. Farewell! I wronged you first; I forgive you. Your hand?

GABRIEL: Here it is.

They shake hands. The sound of others approaching gets louder. Antonio gestures to Gabriel to flee. Gabriel hesitates a moment and then leaves.

ANTONIO: But that was the hand of a woman! (Woman or devil, he certainly set me straight!) . . But I must take care not to let others know of this misadventure, because then I would be ridiculed and disgraced. I have just enough strength to reach my lodgings. What a miserable carnival for me! . . . (*Laboriously drags himself to the Colosseum, where he disappears beneath the arcades.*)

Scene 3

Astolphe, Tutor.

ASTOLPHE (*in a blue domino, mask in his hand*): I trust you. Gabrielle has told me a hundred times that you were an honest man. If you were to betray me . . . What does it matter? I cannot be unhappier than I am now.

TUTOR: I came to much the same conclusion. Were your plan to be devious, to betray me and inform the Prince that you and I have dealings, I could not be in a worse position with him than I already am. For by now, he cannot doubt that instead of trying to put Gabriel back into his clutches, I search for Gabriel only so that he may escape pursuit.

ASTOLPHE: Alas! While we look for her here, Gabrielle might already have fallen into his clutches. Senseless old man! What does he hope to gain by carrying her off like that? The captivity could not change anything in our respective positions; nor could it last long. Does he hope to be spared the common lot of man by living longer than nature dictates?

TUTOR: The doctors were sure he would be dead six months before now. But we near the end of winter. If he withstands the cold spells, he may well live through the summer.

ASTOLPHE: We need to find out where Gabrielle is either hiding or being held captive. If she is a captive, then count on me to deliver her promptly.

TUTOR: May God hear you! You know that if Gabriel is not found soon, the Prince intends to charge you with murder before the Grand Council.

ASTOLPHE: The threat would be certain proof for me that he was detaining Gabriel. The cowardly brute!

TUTOR: My fears are even greater . . .

ASTOLPHE: Do not tell me. I have been disheartened enough over the past three months of searching for her in vain.

TUTOR: My dear Lord Astolphe, are you trying as hard as you can to find her?

ASTOLPHE (*bitterly*): Do you doubt it?

TUTOR: Alas! Here you are in a mask, roaming about the carnival, as if enjoyment were the purpose . . .

ASTOLPHE: You tutors of children are always quick to reprove, and take not the time to think first. Would it not be more reasonable to suppose that I wear a mask and roam the city the more easily to blend in as I search? The carnival has always been a propitious event for lovers, jealous people, and thieves.

TUTOR: Bare your entire soul to me, Lord Astolphe. Is Gabrielle as dear to you now as in the first days of your union?

ASTOLPHE: My God! What have I done to make anyone doubt it? Do you seek to make me feel worse?

TUTOR: God forbid! But it seemed to me, during our many conversations, that mixed in with your affection for her were thoughts of another kind.

ASTOLPHE: Such as?

TUTOR: Do not be angry with me. You know that I am determined to do all that I can for you. But I cannot offer you my ecclesiastical and legal assistance unless I am absolutely certain that there is nothing to which Gabrielle will object later on. You wish to contract in secret a legitimate marriage with your cousin. Given my religious principles, I can only approve of such a resolution. But, since I must consider everything and examine all things from every perspective, I am a little surprised that you, who do not believe in the sanctity of the Church, have thought to initiate this engagement, which you say was never Gabrielle's idea, and to which you would have me make her consent.

ASTOLPHE: Father Chiavari, you know that I am sincere. I cannot hide the truth, since you ask . . . I am horribly jealous. I was unjust and got carried away, I made Gabrielle suffer, and you have received my entire confession on that subject. She left in order to punish me for an insulting suspicion. Yet she forgave me, and she still loves me, for she has mysteriously employed several ingenious ways to keep my hope and confidence alive. This note that I received only last week, containing the single word "Hope!," was definitely in her handwriting, the ink still fresh. So Gabrielle is here! Oh! Yes, I hope! I will find her again soon; I will make her forget my wrongs. But as you know, man is weak. I might wrong Gabrielle again; I do not wish her able to leave me so easily. The trials are too cruel. I feel that some authority, legitimated by a solemn vow on her part, would be my safeguard against her reactions of proud dignity and independence.

TUTOR: So you would be the master? If I had advice to give you, I would dissuade you. I know Gabriel. (They wanted me to make her a man. I succeeded only too well. Never will he tolerate a master.) What you do not obtain through persuasion, you will never obtain. It was high time my tutelage came to an end. Take my word: do not expect me to resume it, and above all, do not try to take it upon yourself. Gabriel would only do once more what he has already done with us both. He would withdraw neither his affection nor his esteem for you, but he would leave you one fine morning like an eagle bursting from the sparrow's cage in which he has been locked.

ASTOLPHE: A vow would be an unbreakable bond for Gabrielle, even though she is hardly more devout than I.

TUTOR: Then he has never made one to you?

ASTOLPHE: She swore her eternal fidelity to me with heaven as a witness.

TUTOR: If he made that vow, then he has kept it, and will always keep it.

ASTOLPHE: But she did not swear obedience to me.

TUTOR: If he did not want to, then he will not want to, and will never want to.

ASTOLPHE: But she must, I will make her.

TUTOR: I do not think so.

ASTOLPHE: You forget that I have the means. I have control over her secret.

TUTOR: You will never abuse that; you said so.

ASTOLPHE: I will threaten her.

TUTOR: You will not frighten him. He knows well that you will not wish to dishonor the family and name that you both share.

ASTOLPHE: It is a prejudice to believe that the fathers' sins are visited on their children.

TUTOR: But the prejudice holds sway wherever you go.

ASTOLPHE: Gabrielle and I are above such a prejudice.

TUTOR: So your intention is to unveil the secret of his sex?

ASTOLPHE: Unless Gabrielle and I are united by eternal bonds.

TUTOR: In that case, he will give in. For I am certain that what he dreads most in the world is to be relegated by force of law to the condition of a slave.

ASTOLPHE: You are the one, Father Chiavari, who put into her head all these foolish notions. I cannot conceive why you conducted her education in this manner. You have forged in her very being an endless source of pain. An honest and educated man like you should have disillusioned her early on, and thwarted the aims of the old Prince.

TUTOR: It is a crime I repent, and nothing will ease my remorse for it. But the measures were so well taken, and the pupil so eagerly took the bait, that I came to delude even myself and to believe that this impossible destiny could be realized just as his grandfather planned it.

ASTOLPHE: And perhaps as well, you found it pleasant to undertake a philosophical experiment. Well then, what have you discovered? That the same upbringing can provide a woman with as much logic, knowledge, and courage as a man?)But you would not prevent her from having a more tender heart, or from caring more about love than chimerical ambitions. The heart escaped you, Father Chiavari; you fashioned only the mind.

TUTOR: And that is why you should forever respect and revere that mind! Listen, I am going to tell you something rash, outrageous, and that goes against my professed faith and religious duties. Do not contract a marriage with Gabrielle. Let her live and die in disguise, happy and free by your side. As the heir to a great fortune, he will share it with you equally. As a chaste and loyal lover, she will be bound from within by your love for each other, though she be free.

ASTOLPHE: Ah! If you think I still care about my claim to that fortune, then you are wrong and you insult me. As a younger man, I needed to spend lavishly. In two years I squandered the little my father had possessed, of which his own father's hatred could not deprive him. I was eager to throw away the paltry remnants of a bygone grandeur. The idea pleased me to become an adventurer, a sort of pleasure-seeking vagabond, and to sleep, stripped of everything, at the doorstep of palaces that bore the illustrious name of my ancestors. Gabriel came to find me, and by paying my debts, he saved my honor and his own. I accepted his gifts without false delicacy; I saw for myself just how much his noble soul scorned money. But when he paid for all my extravagant spending while he himself engaged in none of it, I thought to correct myself, and I began to grow weary of debauchery. Then, I discovered in this gracious companion a ravishingly beautiful woman, and I adored and dreamed only of her . . . She was ready then to give me back all that was rightfully mine. She wished it. Because we had lived chastely like brother and sister for several months, she had no idea that I could have claims on her other than those of friendship. But I aspired to her love. My love absorbed my entire being. I no longer understood anything of the words "power," "wealth," and "glory," which had sometimes caused me to brood in secret. I even ceased to feel resentment. I was ready to bless old Jules for having formed this being so superior to her sex, who filled my soul with an eternal love and was ready to share it. As soon as I had hopes of becoming her lover, I no longer had any thought, any desire for anyone but her. And when it happened, my very being was overwhelmed by such happiness that I became indifferent to all the privations of poverty. For several more months she lived with my family, and neither one of us thought of turning to our grandfather's fortune. Gabrielle passed for my wife. We thought that it could go on that way forever, that the Prince would forget us, and that we would need nothing beyond the very limited wealth that my mother assumed was all we had.

We were too exhilarated to perceive that we were dependent and surrounded by ill will. When we made this painful discovery, we thought of fleeing to a foreign country, and working to live, safe from all persecution. But Gabrielle feared poverty for me, and I feared it for her. She also had the idea of reconciling me with her grandfather so I could partake of his generosity. She tried without my knowledge, to no avail. So she came back, and every year, for the past three years, you have seen her spend a few weeks at the castle of Bramante, and months at a time in Florence or Pisa. But the rest of the year was spent in the heart of Calabria, in a safe and charming retreat, where our lives would have been enviable, had I not been overpowered by a sinister jealousy, a vague and consuming anxiety, a nameless evil that I cannot explain to myself. You know the rest. I am guilty and unhappy, but surely you realize that greed has nothing to do with my anguish and erring ways.

TUTOR: I pity you, noble Astolphe, and would give my life to restore your lost happiness. But it seems to me that you take the wrong path in wishing to chain Gabrielle's fate to yours. Think how difficult such a marriage would be, how illusory its stability. You could never let society know of it without divulging the truth of Gabrielle's sex. And if that happens, Gabrielle will be able to get out of it, for you are close relatives, and if the Pope refuses to accord you a dispensation, your marriage will be annulled

ASTOLPHE: That is true. But Prince Jules will be no more, and then what great difficulty do you see in Gabrielle's proclaiming her sex?

TUTOR: She will not consent to it willingly! You can force her to, and perhaps, owing to the greatness of her soul, she will not break all her ties with you. But you, young man, will have obtained her hand through a sort of transaction with her, by a verbal or tacit promise not to unveil her sex. You will be coercing her through the very agreement.

ASTOLPHE: God forbid, sir! I am sorry you believe me capable of such a despicable act. It is true that when carried away by my jealousy, I contemplate exposing Gabrielle so that she will have to be mine. But, from the moment she is my wife, I will never do so without her consent.

TUTOR: But how can you know that, poor Astolphe? Jealousy is a devastating affliction with consequences you do not foresee. The title of husband will not give you any more security with Gabrielle than the role of lover. And then, in a new burst of anger and distrust, you will want to force her publicly into that very submission she had agreed to in private.

ASTOLPHE: If I thought myself capable of ever going that far, I would give up my search for Gabrielle immediately, and I would banish myself forever from her presence.

TUTOR: Concentrate for now on finding him, primarily to save him from the dangers he is in. Afterward, you will focus on how to love him with an affection worthy of you both.

ASTOLPHE: You are right, let us resume our search; let us go our separate ways. While I mingle with the crowd trying to find my fugitive on this day of festivities, you explore the cover of deserted areas, where sometimes people who try to escape detection become less cautious and roam freely. What is that under your coat?

TUTOR: (*puts Mosca down, on the street*): I had this little dog brought from Florence. I count on him to find the person we seek. Gabriel raised him, and the animal had a marvelous instinct for finding him when the mischievous boy escaped my lessons to go off into the park and read. If Mosca can pick up his scent, I am quite sure he will not lose it. Look, he is sniffing . . . He is going that way. (*Points to the Colosseum.*) I shall follow him. One need not be blind to be led by a dog.

They separate.

Scene 4

In front of a cabaret. Eleven o'clock at night.
Tables are arranged under an awning, decorated
with garlands of leaves and colored paper lanterns.

Groups of masqueraders pass by on the street; musical instruments can be heard now and then.

Astolphe in a blue domino and Faustina in a pink domino sit at a small table eating sorbets. Their masks are on the table. Gabriel, unrecognizable in a mask and black domino, sits at a nearby table, reading a document.

FAUSTINA (*to Astolphe*): If your conversation remains this lively, I warn you I shall soon tire of it.

ASTOLPHE: Wait, I have more to tell you.

FAUSTINA: Since when do I follow your orders? You will have to follow mine if you want to get a single word out of me.

ASTOLPHE: So you refuse to tell me what business brought Antonio to Rome? Obviously you do not know, because you so enjoy speaking ill of people. If you really knew something, you would not need me to ask you twice.

FAUSTINA: If Antonio is to be believed, then what I know should be of utmost interest to you.

ASTOLPHE: The devil! Speak, you snake! (*Grabs her by the arm.*)

FAUSTINA: Kindly do not crumple my oversleeve. It is of the most delicate lace. Ah! Fickle though he is, Antonio is still the finest lover I have had, and I would not get such a gift from you.

Gabriel begins to listen.

ASTOLPHE (*puts his arm around her waist*): My little Faustina, if you tell me, I will give you a dress and everything that goes with it. Since you are still pretty as an angel, you will look marvelous in it.

FAUSTINA: And with what will you buy me this beautiful dress? With your cousin's money? (*Astolphe strikes the table with his fist.*) Do you realize how very convenient it is, having a rich little cousin to exploit?

ASTOLPHE: Shut your mouth, you scum of the earth, and get out of here! You fill me with disgust!

FAUSTINA: Insulting me now? Good! You will know nothing. And I was going to tell you all.

ASTOLPHE: Very well, what price must I pay before you tattle on him? (*Takes out a purse and puts it on the table.*)

FAUSTINA: How much is in your purse?

ASTOLPHE: Two hundred louis . . . But if that is not enough . . .

A beggar appears.

FAUSTINA: Since you are so generous, allow me to perform a good deed at your expense! (*Throws the purse to the beggar.*)

ASTOLPHE: Since you scorn that sum so much, keep your secret! I am not rich enough to pay for it.

FAUSTINA: So you are ruined again, my poor Astolphe? Well! I have made a fortune. Look! (*Pulls a purse from her pocket.*) I want to refund your two hundred louis. I was wrong to throw it to the poor. Let me pay for that act of charity. It will bring me good luck, and might even bring my unfaithful lover back to me.

ASTOLPHE (*pushes the purse away with revulsion*): Then he is here for a woman? You are sure of it?

FAUSTINA: Much too sure!

ASTOLPHE: Maybe you even know her?

FAUSTINA: Ah! There is the rub! Order us more sorbet, if you still have anything left to pay for it.

At Astolphe's sign, a tray with sorbets and liqueur is brought to the table.

ASTOLPHE: I still have the means to pay for your information, even if I must sell my body to medical students. Speak . . . (*Pours himself some liqueur and drinks distractedly.*)

FAUSTINA: Sell your body for a secret? All right, then! The idea is charming: all I want from you is one night of love. Does that surprise you? Listen, Astolphe, I am no longer a courtesan. I am rich and a woman in love. Is that not what they call it? I have always loved you. Come finish off the carnival in my boudoir.

ASTOLPHE: Strange girl! So for once in your life you will give yourself for nothing? (*Drinks.*)

FAUSTINA: Better than that. I will be the one to pay, because I will tell you Antonio's secret! Are you coming? (*Gets up.*)

ASTOLPHE (*gets up*): If I believed it, I could offer you a bouquet of flowers and serenade you beneath your windows.

FAUSTINA: I do not ask you to be gallant. Just act as if you loved me. Alas, to be loved is a dream I have sometimes had!

ASTOLPHE: Miserable creature! I could have loved you! Because I was a child and did not know what a woman like you was . . . You lie when you express such a regret.

FAUSTINA: Oh! Astolphe, I do not lie. Let my whole life be blamed on judgment day, except for this moment and these words I say to you, "I love you!"

ASTOLPHE: You? . . . Like a fool, I listen to you, torn between tender feelings and disgust!

FAUSTINA: Astolphe, you do not know what a courtesan's passion is. Few men do, for you have to be poor. I have just thrown the last of your money in the street. You cannot be suspicious of me; I could earn five hundred sequins tonight. Look, here is the proof. (*Takes a note from her pocket and presents it to him.*)

ASTOLPHE (*reads*): A splendid offer from a cardinal at the very least.

FAUSTINA: It is from Monsignor Gafrani.

ASTOLPHE: And you refused it?

FAUSTINA: Yes, I saw you pass by in the street, and I sent word for you to join me here. Ah! You were quite moved to learn that a woman was asking for you! You thought you would find the woman of your dreams. But at least you are on her track now, because I know where she is.

ASTOLPHE: You know! What do you know?

FAUSTINA: Did she not come from Calabria?

ASTOLPHE: Oh furies! . . . Who told you that?

FAUSTINA: Antonio. When he is drunk, he likes to brag to me about his conquests.

ASTOLPHE: But her name! Did he dare pronounce her name?

FAUSTINA: I do not know her name. See, I am not lying to you. But if you want, I shall pretend to admire his triumph, and generously offer him my boudoir for his first rendez-vous. I know he is obliged to take many precautions, because the lady is of high rank. He will be delighted at the opportunity to bring her to a safe and pleasant place.

ASTOLPHE: And he will not be wary of your offer?

FAUSTINA: He is so vulgar, he believes that with a little money anything can be arranged . . .

ASTOLPHE (*hides his face in his hands and falls back into his chair*): My God! My God! My God!

FAUSTINA: Well, have you made up your mind, Astolphe?

ASTOLPHE: What about you? Have you made up your mind to hide me in your alcove when they come, and to put up with all the consequences of my rage?

FAUSTINA: You want to kill your mistress? Very well then, as long as you do not spare your rival.

ASTOLPHE: But he is rich, Faustina, and I have nothing.

FAUSTINA: But I hate him. I love you.

ASTOLPHE (*in a state of confusion*): Is this then a dream? The pure woman whom I worshipped, prostrate, my head in the dust, falls into infamy, while the courtesan I trampled under my feet rises up purified by love! Well then! Faustina, I will bathe you in a blood that washes away your sins! . . . The pact is made.

FAUSTINA: Then come and sign it. We do not have a deal if you do not spend tonight in my arms! Well then! What are you doing?

ASTOLPHE (*gulps down several glasses of liqueur*): I must get drunk enough first, you see, to make myself believe that I love you.

FAUSTINA: Always insulting me! Never mind, I will put up with anything. Come along! (*Takes his glass away and leads him off.*)

Astolphe follows her with a distracted air and stops, distraught, at every step. As soon as they have gone, Gabriel, who had gradually come closer and observed them behind the awning, leaves his hiding place and unmasks himself.

GABRIEL (*in black domino, mask in hand, as Astolphe and Faustina reach the end of the street*): I will run and block his path, I will not let him commit a sacrilege! . . . (*Starts forward and stops.*) But to show myself to that prostitute, to bicker over my beloved! . . . My pride will not allow it . . . Oh Astolphe! . . . your jealousy is your excuse. But this moment just destroyed forever what was sacred about our love! . . .

ASTOLPHE (*retraces his steps*): Wait for me, Faustina; I forgot my sword back there.

Gabriel places a folded paper in the hilt of Astolphe's sword, puts his mask back on, and flees, while Astolphe comes back under the awning.

ASTOLPHE (*takes his sword from the table*): Another note telling me once more to hope, perhaps! (*Yanks out the piece of paper, throws it on the ground, and tries to grind it under his foot.*)

Faustina, who has followed him, retrieves the paper and unfolds it.

FAUSTINA: A love letter? On such a large page, and with such big writing? Impossible! What! The Pope's signature! What the devil does His Holiness have to do with you?

ASTOLPHE: What are you saying! Give me back that paper!

FAUSTINA: Oh! This looks too amusing! I want to see what it is and read it to you. (*Reads.*) "We, by the grace of God and the election of the sacred college, spiritual head of the Catholic Church, apostolic and Roman . . . successor of Saint Peter and vicar of Jesus Christ on earth, temporal lord of the Roman states, etc., permit Jules Achille Gabriel of Bramante, grandson, heir apparent and legitimate successor of the very illustrious and very excellent Prince Jules of Bramante, Count of, etc., Lord of, etc. . . . to contract, at the discretion of his conscience or before whichever priest and confessor he deems appropriate, the vow of poverty, chastity, and humility, to authorize him by the present letter to enter a monastery or to live freely in the world, according to whether he feels called upon to work out his salvation in either of these two ways; as well as to authorize him by this letter to transmit, immediately upon the death of his illustrious grandfather, Jules de Bramante, the immediate possession, legal and incontestable, of all his wordly belongings and titles to his legitimate heir Octave-Astolphe of Bramante, son of Octave of Bramante and first cousin of Gabriel of Bramante, upon whom we have bestowed that license and that promise, in order to give him the spiritual peace and freedom of conscience necessary to contract, privately or publicly, a vow upon which, he has declared to us, depends the salvation of his soul. In pledge of which we have delivered to him this authorization signed with our signature and our Pontifical Seal . . ." Well now! What a charming style the Holy Father has! You see, Astolphe? It contains everything! So! Does not that cheer you up? Now you are rich, now you are the Prince of Bramante! . . . Really, it does not surprise me. The poor child was devout and fearful as a woman . . . I say, he did the right thing. Now you can kill Antonio and carry me off with the "spiritual peace and discretion of your conscience."

ASTOLPHE (*grabs the sheet of paper from her*): If you were counting on that, you were mistaken. (*Tears up the paper and burns the pieces with a candle.*)

FAUSTINA (*bursts into laughter*): What a Don Quixote! So you will never change?

ASTOLPHE (*to himself*): To repair such wrongs, whitewash such an insult, close up such a wound with gold and titles . . . Ah! One must have sunk low indeed to dare console me in such a manner.

FAUSTINA: What are you talking about? What! Your cousin also . . . (*Makes a meaningful gesture on Astolphe's forehead.*)[31] I see that your Calabrian lady had some experience before Antonio came along.

---

[31] Faustina makes the flippant gesture of the "horned hand." In France and Italy, as in many other countries, a man betrayed by his wife is said to be wearing the horns of a cuckold on his head.

ASTOLPHE (*pays no attention to Faustina*): Do I need this insulting concession? Oh! Nothing will stop me now. I know well how to assert my rights . . . I will unmask the imposture, expose their shame for all to see . . . Antonio will be called to witness . . .

FAUSTINA: But what do you mean? I do not understand your words! You seem out of your mind! Listen to me and come to your senses!

ASTOLPHE: What do you want from me? Leave me alone, I am neither rich nor a prince. I take it your whim has passed?

FAUSTINA: On the contrary, I wait for you!

ASTOLPHE: Indeed! Women appear to be practicing extraordinary selflessness this year. Great ladies and prostitutes alike prefer their lover to their fortune. If this goes on for much longer, we shall be able to put them all on the same level.

FAUSTINA (*notices Gabriel, who has reappeared*): Now there is a rather curious fellow!

ASTOLPHE: Maybe he is the one who delivered the note? . . . (*Kisses Faustina.*) He will see that tonight I am not at all for serious matters. Come, my dear Fausta. By your side, I am the happiest of men.

Gabriel disappears. Astolphe and Faustina prepare to leave.

Scene 5

Antonio, Faustina, Astolphe.

Antonio, pale and barely able to stand, appears as they are about to leave.

FAUSTINA (*cries out and recoils, terrified*): Is that a ghost?

ASTOLPHE: Ah! The heavens sent him to me! Woe betide him! . . .

ANTONIO (*in a faint voice*): What are you saying? It is I, Antonio. Help me, I faint again. (*Throws himself onto a bench.*)

FAUSTINA: He is leaving a trail of blood! How awful! What does this mean? Did someone try to kill you, Antonio?

ANTONIO: No. Wounded in a duel . . . badly . . .

FAUSTINA: Astolphe! Call for help . . .

ANTONIO: No, for pity's sake! . . . Do not do that . . . I do not want anyone to know . . . Give me a little water! . . . (*Astolphe gives him a glass of water. Faustina makes him breathe smelling salts.*) I feel revived.

ASTOLPHE: We will bring you back to your place. Surely someone is there who can take better care of you than we can.

ANTONIO: Thank you. I will take your arm. Let me work up some strength . . . If this bleeding would only stop . . .

FAUSTINA (*gives him a handkerchief, which he puts on his chest*): Poor Antonio! Your lips are so blue . . . Come to my place . . .

ANTONIO: You are a good girl, all the more so as I treated you badly. But I shall no more . . . Go, I was quite ridiculous . . . Astolphe, since we meet here, when I thought you were far away, I wish to tell you . . . because your cousin . . . will tell you what this is all about, and I would just as soon be the first to accuse myself . . .

ASTOLPHE: My male cousin or my female cousin?

ANTONIO: Ah! So you know of my folly? He already told you . . . It cost me dearly! I was convinced that he was a woman . . .

FAUSTINA: What is he talking about?

ANTONIO: His method of proving me wrong was brutally persuasive: a terrible thrust of his sword in my side . . . At first I thought it was not serious; I tried to go home alone. But as I crossed the Colosseum, I fell unconscious and lay there in a faint for . . . I know not how long! . . . What time is it?

FAUSTINA: Almost midnight.

ANTONIO: Eight bells had just rung when I met Gabriel de Bramante behind the Colosseum.

ASTOLPHE (*as if coming out of a dream*): Gabriel! My cousin! You fought with him! And did you kill him?

ANTONIO: I never even scratched him, and his last thrust I shall not forget for a long time . . . (*Drinks some water.*) The bleeding has let up a bit . . . Ah! What a fellow he is! . . . I think I can get back to my lodging now . . . Help me a little, both of you . . . I will tell you the whole story.

ASTOLPHE (*aside*): Is this a ploy? Would he stoop that low? . . . (*Aloud.*) Then you are truly wounded? (*Looks at Antonio's chest. Aside.*) Indeed, the wound is large. Oh Gabrielle! (*Aloud.*) I will get you a surgeon . . . as soon as I have taken you home . . .

FAUSTINA: No! My place, it is closer.

> *They exit, supporting Antonio on each side.*

Scene 6

A small dark room. Gabriel, Marc.

Gabriel, in black, with his domino thrown back over his shoulders, sits in a dreamy pose, lost in thought. Marc upstage.

MARC: It is two o'clock in the morning, my lord. Do you not think it time to lie down?

GABRIEL: Go to sleep, my friend. I no longer need anything.

MARC: Alas! You will fall ill! Believe me, it would be better for you to make up with Lord Astolphe, since you cannot forget him . . .

GABRIEL: Leave, my good Marc. I assure you I feel at peace.

MARC: But if I leave, you will not retire. Tomorrow morning I will find you here, sitting in the same place, your lamp still burning. One day your hair will catch fire . . . and if that does not happen, you will finally die of grief. If you could see how you have changed!

GABRIEL: So much the better. My fresh complexion betrayed my sex. Now that I am a boy forever, it is fitting that my cheeks are hollowed out . . . Why do you keep looking at that door?

MARC: You did not hear something? A scratching sound at the door.

GABRIEL: It is your sword. You insist on being armed all the time, even in your own bedroom.

MARC: I will not be at ease until you make peace with your grandfather . . . Listen! Again!

A scratching sound and small groan are heard at the door.

GABRIEL (*walks to the door*): It is some animal . . . That is not a human sound. (*About to open the door.*)

MARC (*stops him*): In heaven's name! Let me open it first, and draw your sword . . .

Gabriel opens the door despite Marc's efforts to prevent him. Mosca enters and jumps at Gabriel's legs, yelping with joy.

GABRIEL: Well, no cause for worry here! A dog no bigger than your fist! So! It is my poor Mosca! How was he able to find me from so far away? Poor loving creature! (*Takes Mosca on his knees and pets him.*)

MARC: Now I am anxious indeed . . . Mosca could not have come here on his own, someone must have brought him . . . Prince Jules is here!

Knocking heard below. Marc grabs pistols from the table.

GABRIEL: Whatever it is, Marc, I forbid you to risk your life by putting up a fight. You see, I no longer care about mine . . . Whatever happens, I shall not defend myself. I have struggled enough to end up where I am, and it was not worth the trouble. (*Looks down through the window.*) One man by himself? . . . Go speak to him through the grating. Find out what he wants. But if it is Astolphe, I forbid you to let him in. (*Marc exits.*) So who led you to me, my poor Mosca? Would an enemy have generously sent the only being who remained faithful to me even during my absence?

MARC (*comes back*): It is Father Chiavari. He wishes to have a word with you. But do not trust him, my lord. He may have been sent by your grandfather.

GABRIEL (*leaving*): Better a hundred times over to suffer disloyalty than to betray a friendship. I will go to meet him.

MARC: Let us see if anyone has followed him in the street. (*Loads his pistols and looks out the window.*) No, no one.

Scene 7

Tutor, Gabriel, Marc.

TUTOR: Oh, my dear child! My noble Gabriel! Thank you for not distrusting me. Alas! How tired and sad you look!

MARC: Quite so, Father. I was saying that just now.

GABRIEL: What a good servant! His devotion is ever the same. Go lie down, my friend. I shall call you to escort Father Chiavari when he is ready to leave.

MARC: I go because you order me to. But I cannot sleep. (*Exits.*)

TUTOR: Oh, poor little Mosca! He took me all over the place! From the Colosseum, where he picked up your scent, to here, he had me walk all evening. First he led me to the Vatican . . . then to a cabaret near the Piazza Navona. By then I had given up hope of finding you. Even he lay down, worn out, when suddenly he gave the little yelp you know and took off. He was so insistent at your door that I took a chance and passed him through the grating.

GABRIEL: I love him a hundred times more for leading my friend to me. But what brings you to Rome, dear Father?

TUTOR: A wish to help and a fear that misfortune will befall you.

GABRIEL: My grandfather is quite angry?

TUTOR: As you can imagine. But you are well hidden, and now you are surrounded by trusted guardians. Astolphe is here.

GABRIEL: I am well aware of that.

TUTOR: I conferred with him. I wanted to know if this man was truly attached to you . . . He loves you, I am sure of it.

GABRIEL: I know all that, but do not speak to me of him.

TUTOR: But I do wish to speak to you of him, because his repentance calls for your forgiveness.

GABRIEL: Oh, I know how much he repents.

TUTOR: Only an excess of love could have driven him to make the mistakes for which your departure punished him too severely.

GABRIEL: Listen, my friend, I know better than you every single word, act, and thought that is Astolphe's. For three months, I have hovered around him like his shadow. I have observed his every action, and even heard word for word the long conversations the two of you had . . .

TUTOR: What! You knew I was here, and you did not dare confide in me?

GABRIEL: Forgive me. Unhappiness causes one to retreat.

TUTOR: And were you there when we were at the Colosseum tonight?

GABRIEL: No, but I listened to you last week at the Baths of Diocletian. I was at the Colosseum tonight, but only met Antonio Vezzonila. I quarreled with him because he had just about guessed my sex. I do not know if he will die from the blow of my sword. In any other circumstance, he would have taken my life. But I had something to accomplish, and fate was on my side. I was playing my last card. I beat the unlucky obstacle that had crossed my path. He is yet another victim on whom Astolphe will lay the foundations of his fortune.

TUTOR: I do not understand you, my child!

GABRIEL: Astolphe will explain it all tomorrow morning. Tomorrow I leave Rome.

TUTOR: With him, surely?

GABRIEL: No, my friend. I am leaving Astolphe forever.

TUTOR: Can you not forgive? It is yourself whom you punish cruelly.

GABRIEL: I know, and I forgive him in my heart what I am going to suffer. The day will come when I shall be able to extend a fraternal hand to him. Today I could not bear to see him.

TUTOR: Let me bring him to your feet: even though it is late, I know that I shall find him still up and about; he put on a disguise to go look for you.

GABRIEL: At this hour, he does not look for me. I am better informed than you, my dear tutor. While you listen to what he says, I hear what he really thinks. Listen carefully to what I am telling you. Astolphe does not love me anymore. The very first time he insulted me with an unjustified suspicion, I understood that he was cursing love, because his heart had wearied of loving. For a long time I pushed away this dreadful conviction. I can no longer stave it off. Doubt opened the way to ingratitude in Astolphe's heart. And the more he killed our love with distrust, the more other passions gradually took possession of him, and replaced his dying passion for me, almost unbeknownst to him. Today his love is nothing more than a savage pride, a thirst for vengeance and control. His selflessness is no more than an unfulfilled ambition that scorns money only to the extent that it aspires to better . . . Do not defend him! I know he still deludes himself, and that he has not yet coldly meditated the crime he wishes to commit. But I also know that his inaction and obscurity weigh heavily upon him. He is a man! He could not be content with a life devoted exclusively to love and contemplation. When we lived alone together, he dreamed over and over, against his own will, of what would have been his role in the world if our grandfather had not preferred me to him. And today, while planning to marry me and proclaim my sex, what he really has in mind is not so much the assurance of my fidelity as the chance to regain a brilliant place in society, a great title, political rights—in a word: power, of which men are more jealous than money. I know that only yesterday, perhaps this morning still, he struggled against the temptation and quailed at the very idea of despicable acts. But tomorrow, or perhaps this evening, he may already have crossed that line, and the paltriest bait swung at his jealousy will serve as a pretext to trample his love underfoot and listen to his ambition. I saw the gathering storm. To protect his honor from a crime and my freedom from a yoke, I found an expedient. I went to the Pope, feigned exalted Christian piety, and declared that I wanted to live in celibacy. I obtained from him an order that Astolphe would take my place upon the death of my grandfather, so that my inheritance would stay within the family. The Pope listened to me with kindness. He obligingly took into account my grandfather's prejudice against Astolphe and the necessity to accommodate that prejudice. He promised to keep the secret and gave me a guarantee for the future. The order, signed this very evening, is already in Astolphe's hands.

TUTOR: Astolphe will never make use of it, and will come tear it up at your feet. Do let me go get him. It is possible that your perceptions are accurate, and that the day will come when you must steel yourself with great courage and inflexible rigor. But until then, should you not try every means to raise up that battered soul and regain the happiness so dearly fought for up to now? Love, my child, is more serious in my eyes (in the eyes of a poor priest who has never experienced it!) than in the eyes of any man I have met in my lifetime. I would almost say to all those who are loved what the Lord said to his disciples: "These souls are in your care." No, you cannot have possessed the soul of another without assuming sacred duties toward it. One day you will have to give an account to God for the sins or merits of that troubled soul of which you yourself became the judge, the arbiter, and the divinity! Use all your influence, then, to pull that soul from the abyss into which it strays. Fulfill that task as a duty, and do not abandon it until you have exhausted every means to lift it up.

GABRIEL: You are right, Father; you speak like a Christian, but not like a man! You do not know that when love has been one's guiding force, it cannot be replaced by reason or morality. The power that one had was the very love that one felt; a faith and enthusiasm that gave one the power and made it invincible. When such love becomes Christian charity or philosophical eloquence, it loses all its power; the work begun with intense fervor cannot be completed in cool detachment. The ability to persuade Astolphe is no longer in me, because I feel that the purpose of my life is no longer to persuade him. His soul has fallen beneath mine. If I raised it up, then it would be the work of my own doing. I might love him the way you love me, but no longer would I be bowing down in adoration before the fully realized being, the ideal that God had created for me. Know this, my friend: love cannot be other than the belief that one's beloved is a superior being; once that belief is crushed, nothing remains but friendship.

TUTOR: Friendship still imposes strict duties and makes heroic deeds possible. You cannot forswear love and friendship all in the same day!

GABRIEL: I respect your opinion. But give me the rest of the night to reflect on what you ask me. Give me your word that you will not tell Astolphe where to find me.

TUTOR: I give you my word, if you give me yours not to leave Rome without seeing me one more time. I shall come back tomorrow morning.

GABRIEL: Yes, my friend, I promise. The streets are not safe this late at night. Let Marc escort you.

TUTOR: No, my child, it is carnival night and half the world is still awake. There is no danger. Marc has probably fallen asleep. Do not awaken the dear old fellow. Until tomorrow! May God give you counsel! . . .

GABRIEL: May God be with you! Until tomorrow!

Tutor exits. Gabriel sees him to the door and returns.

Scene 8

GABRIEL (*alone*): Reflect? Reflect on what? On the extent of my unhappiness? On how impossible it is to remedy? At this very hour, Astolphe forgets everything in his shameless drunken transports! And I, how could I ever forget that his breast, the sanctuary where I once rested my head, was profaned by impure embraces? What! From now on, each of his suspicions will have the power to bring on his need for base pleasures, and make him feel entitled to defile his lips with the lips of prostitutes! And he wants to defile me as well! He wants to treat me like them! He wants to call me before a court, before an assembly of men, and there, before the judges, before the crowd, have the henchmen tear away my doublet, and for proof of his rights to fortune and power, unveil for all to see the female breast whose trembling he alone has seen! Oh Astolphe, that thought has doubtless not occurred to you. But when the time comes, when you are carried down that fatal slope, you will not be deterred by such a small matter! Well then! I say: Never! I refuse to be subjected to that final outrage. Rather than suffer the affront, I shall rip open my chest, I shall mutilate this breast until I have made it a hideous sight to all those who would gaze upon it, and the sight of my nakedness will bring a smile to no one's face . . . Oh my God! Protect me! Preserve me! I can barely resist the temptation of suicide! . . . (*Falls to her knees and prays.*)

Scene 9

On the Sant'Angelo Bridge.[32] Four o'clock in the morning. Gabriel, followed by Mosca, Giglio.

GABRIEL (*walks agitatedly and stops midway across the bridge*): Suicide! . . . The thought does not leave my mind. Yet I feel better here! . . . I could not breathe in that little room. I feared every moment that my sobs would awaken poor Marc, my faithful servant who grows ever more decrepit as a result of my misfortunes, and whom my sadness has aged more than the passing years! (*Mosca lets out a long howl.*) Quiet, Mosca! I know that you love me too. An old servant and an old dog, that is all I have left! . . . (*Paces a bit.*) The night is beautiful! And the fresh air does some good! . . . O radiant stars! O sweet-sounding murmur of the Tiber! . . . (*Mosca lets out a second howl.*) What is the matter, frail creature? As a child, I was told that when a dog howls three times in the same way,

---

[32] Originally constructed in 134–39 by the Roman emperor Hadrian, the bridge and nearby castle acquired the name Sant'Angelo in the seventh century, when according to legend an angel appeared on the castle roof to announce the end of the plague. In the sixteenth century, the bridge was decorated with the statues of ten angels and in later years was a place where the bodies of the executed were exposed.

it is the harbinger of a death in the family . . . I never thought the day would come when that omen would cause me no fear whatsoever for myself . . . (*Paces a bit more and leans over the parapet.*)

GIGLIO (*hiding in the shadow cast over the bridge by the Sant'Angelo Castle; approaches Gabriel*): That was his lodging, and that is he; I have not lost sight of him once since he came out. That is not the old servant of whom I was told . . . This one is a young man.

Mosca howls a third time and presses close to Gabriel.

GABRIEL: It is indeed the omen. Oh dear God, may it be fulfilled! I know that nothing ever again can give me sadness.

GIGLIO (*comes even closer*): The devil take that dog! Luckily he does not seem to pay any attention to it . . . By the devil! It is so easy that I lack the courage . . . If I did not have a wife and children, I would stay right where I am!

GABRIEL: However, with freedom (and the arrangement I made with the Pope is bound to shield me from every danger), solitude could still be beautiful. What poetry in the contemplation of these stars, poetry that my desire can so freely make its own, without any base passion chaining it to earthly things! O freedom of the soul! Who in their right minds can deny you? (*Stretches his arms to the sky.*) Give me back that freedom, dear God! My soul expands just from uttering that word: freedom! . . .

GIGLIO (*stabs him with his dagger*): There now, straight through the heart!

GABRIEL: Right to the mark, good sir. I asked for freedom, and you gave it to me. (*Falls.*)

Mosca fills the air with his howls.

GIGLIO: Now he is dead. Will you be quiet, wretched beast? (*Tries to grab him; Mosca escapes, barking.*) I cannot catch him! Better hurry up and finish the task. (*Gets closer to Gabriel and tries to lift him up.*) Ah! A rabbit has more courage. I am trembling like a leaf! I was not cut out for this sort of job.

GABRIEL: You would throw me in the Tiber? It is not worth the trouble. Let me die peacefully in the starlight. You can see for yourself that I do not call for help and care not at all about dying.

GIGLIO: Here is a man like me. And now, if it did not mean having to appear before the heavenly judge, I would like to be dead. Ah! Tomorrow I go to confession! . . . But by the devil! I have seen this young man before . . . Yes, it is he! Oh! I could break my head open on the pavement! (*Falls to his knees next to Gabriel and tries to pull the dagger from his breast.*)

GABRIEL: What are you doing, miserable wretch? Why so eager to see me die?

GIGLIO: My master! My angel! . . . My God! If I could bring you back to life.[33] Ah! God of heaven and earth, do not let him die! . . .

GABRIEL: It is too late. What does it matter to you?

GIGLIO (*aside*): He does not recognize me! Ah! So much the better! If he cursed me now, I would be damned forever.

GABRIEL: Whoever you are, I bear you no grudge. You have carried out heaven's will.

GIGLIO: No, I am not a thief. As you see, master, I do not wish to rob you.

GABRIEL: Then who sent you? If it is Astolphe . . . do not tell me . . . Finish me off instead.

GIGLIO: Astolphe? I do not know that name . . .

GABRIEL: Thank you! I die in peace. I know where the blow came from . . . All is well.

GIGLIO: He is dying! God is not just! He is dying! I cannot bring him back to life . . . (*Mosca comes back and licks Gabriel's face and hands.*) Ah! The poor beast has more heart than I do.

GABRIEL: Friend, do not kill my poor dog . . .

GIGLIO: Friend! He calls me friend! (*Beats his head with his fists.*)

---

[33] That Giglio uses *tu* with Gabriel marks his status as a person of low origins who might use *tu* with everybody, but it may also mark a feeling of closeness he feels with Gabriel as the man who once spared him his life.

GABRIEL: Someone may come . . . Go quickly! . . . Why do you stay here? . . . I cannot recover from this. Go collect your wages . . . from my grandfather!

GIGLIO: His grandfather! Ah! So those are the men who hired us! So that is how our princes use us! . . .

GABRIEL: Listen! . . . I do not want my body to be jeered at by passersby . . . Tie a stone to me . . . and throw me into the water . . .

GIGLIO: No! You are still alive, you speak, you can recover. Oh my God! My God! Will no one come to your rescue?

GABRIEL: The agony has lasted too long . . . I am in pain. Pull the dagger from my chest. (*Giglio pulls out dagger.*) Thank you, I feel better . . . I feel . . . free! . . . My dream comes back to me. I feel as if I am soaring upward! So very high aloft! (*Expires.*)

GIGLIO: He breathes no longer! I tried to make him feel better, and hastened his death . . . His wound does not bleed . . . Ah! It is all over with! . . . It was his request . . . to throw him into the river . . . (*Tries to pick up Gabriel's body.*) My strength fails me, my vision is blurred, the road slips and slides beneath my feet! . . . Just God! . . . the angel of the castle is beating his wings and sounding his trumpet . . . It is the voice of the Last Judgment! Ah! Here are the dead, the dead who have come to get me. (*Falls facedown on the pavement and covers his ears.*)

Scene 10

Astolphe, Tutor, Gabriel dead, Giglio lying
on the ground.

ASTOLPHE (*walks*): Well! You are not the one who failed
to keep your promise. I forced you against your will!

TUTOR (*stops, dubious*): I am too weak . . . Gabriel will
never trust me again.

ASTOLPHE (*pulls him along*): I want to see her! To see her!
To kiss her feet. She will forgive me! Lead me to her.

MARC (*comes to meet them, a lantern in one hand, a sword
in the other*): Father, is that you?

TUTOR: Where do you run to, Marc? You seem distraught! Where is your master?

MARC: I am looking for him now! He went out . . . went
out while I slept! Wretched soul that I am! . . . I was on
my way to your place.

TUTOR: I have not come across him . . . But surely he
left armed?

MARC: He left unarmed for the first time in his life, for-
getting even his dagger. Oh! I dare not tell you what I fear.
He was so distressed. For the past few days, he would not
eat, would not sleep, would not read, he would not keep
still for a moment.

ASTOLPHE: Quiet, Marc, you are killing me. Let us look
for him! . . . What do I see here? . . . (*Grabs the lantern*

from Marc and shines it over Giglio.) What is this man doing here?

GIGLIO: Kill me! Kill me!

TUTOR: And here, a body!

MARC (*in a choked voice*): Mosca! . . . here is Mosca licking his hands!

The Tutor falls to his knees. Marc cries and shouts, raises Gabriel's body. Astolphe remains standing, petrified.

GIGLIO (*to the Tutor*): Give me absolution, Father! Gentlemen, kill me. I am the one who killed this young man, a good, noble young man who granted me my life one night after I tried with a band of criminals to rob and murder him. Kill me! I have a wife and children, but it does not matter, I want to die!

ASTOLPHE (*grabs his throat*): Wretch! You murdered him!

TUTOR: Do not kill him. He was not acting on his own. I recognize the doings of the prince of Bramante. I have seen this man at his palace.

GIGLIO: Yes, I was in his service.

ASTOLPHE: And he is the one who ordered you to commit this crime?

GIGLIO: I have a wife and children, sir. I already gave them the money I received. Now deliver me to the authorities. I killed my savior, my master, my Jesus! Send

187

me to the gallows. You can see for yourself I am giving myself up. Father, pray for me!

ASTOLPHE: Ah! Coward, fanatic! I shall crush you to the ground.

TUTOR: The confessions this wretch has made will be valuable. Spare him. Do not doubt for a moment the Prince will immediately have you accused. Courage, Lord Astolphe! You owe it to the memory of the woman who loved you to protect your honor from slander.

ASTOLPHE (*clutches himself in agony*): My honor! What does my honor matter? (*Throws himself on Gabriel's body.*)

Marc pushes him back.

MARC: Leave her in peace now! You are the one who killed her.

ASTOLPHE (*rises with a distracted air*): Yes, I am the one! Yes, it was I! Who dares say otherwise! I am the one who killed her!

TUTOR: Calm yourself and come along! We must shield this sacred corpse from the infamy of public attention. There is still time before daybreak; let us carry her away from here. We shall place her in the nearest convent. We ourselves shall bury her and not leave her until we have hidden in the womb of the earth the secret that she so carefully preserved.

ASTOLPHE: Oh! Yes, may she carry to the tomb that secret I wanted to violate!

TUTOR (*to Giglio*): Come along, since you show salutary signs of remorse. I will try to make your peace with heaven. If you sincerely confess, we can save your life.

GIGLIO: I will confess all, but I want only absolution, not life.

ASTOLPHE (*in frenzied agony*): Yes, you will have absolution, and you will be my friend, my companion! We shall never separate, because we are both murderers!

Marc and Giglio carry the corpse away. The Tutor leads off Astolphe.

END

Works Cited in the Notes

Bishop, Morris. *The Middle Ages*. Boston: Mariner, 2001. Print.

Musacchio, Jacqueline. "The Rape of the Sabine Women on Quattrocento Marriage-Panels." *Marriage in Italy, 1300–1650*. Ed. Trevor Dean and K. J. P. Lowe. Cambridge: Cambridge UP, 1998. 66–84. Print.

Pasco, Allan. "Jouy's *Cécile* and the Narcissistic Romantic Hero." *Echoes of Narcissus*. Ed. Lieve Spaas and Trista Selous. New York: Berghahn, 2000. 247–61. Print.

Poli, Annarosa. *L'Italie dans la vie et dans l'œuvre de George Sand*. Moncalieri: Centro Interuniversitario di Ricerche sul Viaggio in Italia, 2000. Print.

Présences de l'Italie dans l'œuvre de George Sand. Pref. Annarosa Poli. Moncalieri: Centro Interuniversitario di Ricerehe sul Viaggio in Italia, 2004. Print.

Rouget, Marie-Thérèse. *George Sand et l'Italie*. Paris: Jean-Renard, 1939. Print.

Modern Language Association of America
Texts and Translations

Texts

Anna Banti. *"La signorina" e altri racconti.* Ed. and introd. Carol Lazzaro-Weis. 2001.

Bekenntnisse einer Giftmischerin, von ihr selbst geschrieben. Ed. and introd. Raleigh Whitinger and Diana Spokiene. 2009.

Adolphe Belot. *Mademoiselle Giraud, ma femme.* Ed and introd. Christopher Rivers. 2002.

Dovid Bergelson. אָפּגאַנג. Ed. and introd. Joseph Sherman. 1999.

Elsa Bernstein. *Dämmerung: Schauspiel in fünf Akten.* Ed. and introd. Susanne Kord. 2003.

Edith Bruck. *Lettera alla madre.* Ed. and introd. Gabriella Romani. 2006.

Isabelle de Charrière. *Lettres de Mistriss Henley publiées par son amie.* Ed. Joan Hinde Stewart and Philip Stewart. 1993.

Isabelle de Charrière. *Trois femmes: Nouvelle de l'Abbé de la Tour.* Ed. and introd. Emma Rooksby. 2007.

François-Timoléon de Choisy, Marie-Jeanne L'Héritier, and Charles Perrault. *Histoire de la Marquise-Marquis de Banneville.* Ed. Joan DeJean. 2004.

Sophie Cottin. *Claire d'Albe.* Ed. and introd. Margaret Cohen. 2002.

Marceline Desbordes-Valmore. *Sarah.* Ed. Deborah Jenson and Doris Y. Kadish. 2008.

Claire de Duras. *Ourika.* Ed. Joan DeJean. Introd. DeJean and Margaret Waller. 1994.

Şeyh Galip. *Hüsn ü Aşk.* Ed. and introd. Victoria Rowe Holbrook. 2005.

Françoise de Graffigny. *Lettres d'une Péruvienne.* Introd. Joan DeJean and Nancy K. Miller. 1993.

Sofya Kovalevskaya. Нигилистка. Ed. and introd. Natasha Kolchevska. 2001.

Thérèse Kuoh-Moukoury. *Rencontres essentielles.* Introd. Cheryl Toman. 2002.

Juan José Millás. *"Trastornos de carácter" y otros cuentos.* Introd. Pepa Anastasio. 2007.

Emilia Pardo Bazán. *"El encaje roto" y otros cuentos.* Ed. and introd. Joyce Tolliver. 1996.

Rachilde. *Monsieur Vénus: Roman matérialiste.* Ed. and introd. Melanie Hawthorne and Liz Constable. 2004.

Marie Riccoboni. *Histoire d'Ernestine*. Ed. Joan Hinde Stewart and Philip Stewart. 1998.

George Sand. *Gabriel*. Ed. Kathleen Robin Hart. 2010.

Eleonore Thon. *Adelheit von Rastenberg*. Ed. and introd. Karin A. Wurst. 1996.

Translations

Anna Banti. *"The Signorina" and Other Stories*. Trans. Martha King and Carol Lazzaro-Weis. 2001.

Adolphe Belot. *Mademoiselle Giraud, My Wife*. Trans. Christopher Rivers. 2002.

Dovid Bergelson. *Descent*. Trans. Joseph Sherman. 1999.

Elsa Bernstein. *Twilight: A Drama in Five Acts*. Trans. Susanne Kord. 2003.

Edith Bruck. *Letter to My Mother*. Trans. Brenda Webster with Gabriella Romani. 2006.

Isabelle de Charrière. *Letters of Mistress Henley Published by Her Friend*. Trans. Philip Stewart and Jean Vaché. 1993.

Isabelle de Charrière. *Three Women: A Novel by the Abbé de la Tour*. Trans. Emma Rooksby. 2007.

François-Timoléon de Choisy, Marie-Jeanne L'Héritier, and Charles Perrault. *The Story of the Marquise-Marquis de Banneville*. Trans. Steven Rendall. 2004.

Confessions of a Poisoner, Written by Herself. Trans. Raleigh Whitinger and Diana Spokiene. 2009.

Sophie Cottin. *Claire d'Albe*. Trans. Margaret Cohen. 2002.

Marceline Desbordes-Valmore. *Sarah*. Trans. Deborah Jenson and Doris Y. Kadish. 2008.

Claire de Duras. *Ourika*. Trans. John Fowles. 1994.

Şeyh Galip. *Beauty and Love*. Trans. Victoria Rowe Holbrook. 2005.

Françoise de Graffigny. *Letters from a Peruvian Woman*. Trans. David Kornacker. 1993.

Sofya Kovalevskaya. *Nihilist Girl*. Trans. Natasha Kolchevska with Mary Zirin. 2001.

Thérèse Kuoh-Moukoury. *Essential Encounters*. Trans. Cheryl Toman. 2002.

Juan José Millás. *"Personality Disorders" and Other Stories*. Trans. Gregory B. Kaplan. 2007.

Emilia Pardo Bazán. *"Torn Lace" and Other Stories*. Trans. María Cristina Urruela. 1996.

Rachilde. *Monsieur Vénus: A Materialist Novel*. Trans. Melanie Hawthorne. 2004.

Marie Riccoboni. *The Story of Ernestine*. Trans. Joan Hinde Stewart and Philip Stewart. 1998.

George Sand. *Gabriel*. Trans. Kathleen Robin Hart and Paul Fenouillet. 2010.

Eleonore Thon. *Adelheit von Rastenberg*. Trans. George F. Peters. 1996.

Texts and Translations in One-Volume Anthologies

Modern Italian Poetry. Ed. and trans. Ned Condini. Introd. Dana Renga. 2009.

Modern Urdu Poetry. Ed., introd., and trans. M. A. R. Habib. 2003.

Nineteenth-Century Women's Poetry from France. Ed. Gretchen Schultz. Trans. Anne Atik, Michael Bishop, Mary Ann Caws, Melanie Hawthorne, Rosemary Lloyd, J. S. A. Lowe, Laurence Porter, Christopher Rivers, Schultz, Patricia Terry, and Rosanna Warren. 2008.

Nineteenth-Century Women's Poetry from Spain. Ed. Anna-Marie Aldaz. Introd. Susan Kirkpatrick. Trans. Aldaz and W. Robert Walker. 2008.

Spanish American Modernismo. Ed. Kelly Washbourne. Trans. Washbourne with Sergio Waisman. 2007.